Something for Everyone

by
Adell Digby

1-7-2004

For a good Friend

Ann Hodges

Adell Digby

Cork Hill Press
Indianapolis

Cork Hill Press
7520 East 88th Place, Suite 101
Indianapolis, Indiana 46256-1253
1-866-688-BOOK
www.corkhillpress.com

Trade Paperback Edition: 1-59408-196-4

Printed in the United States of America

1 3 5 7 9 10 8 6 4 2

A Promise I Wish I Had Never Kept

A PROMISE I WISH I HAD NEVER KEPT

Walking down that dusty old road that I have walked down so many times before, seems like to me I was walking off into a wild blue yonder, whatever that might mean, since I have heard that phase so many times in my lifetime and still don't know what it means. That must have been the right phase to use. Before I reached the road that our driveway entered into, many things went through my mind. All the rest had gone their own way and found that other world that I knew was waiting out there for me. I gathered myself together and realized that Mom and Dad were getting old and would not be able to take care of me much longer. I was only sixteen years old and had never worked anywhere except with Dad. I knew out there somewhere, must be more than I grew up with. Although we always had plenty of food, plenty to wear and a warm place to live. Dad had a way of taking care of his own and managed to have a little to put aside for that raining day. We had everything we needed to make us happy, but I knew just like the rest that the time had come to get out and find that other world. Oh I knew that I would be coming back to take care of Mom and Dad when it become necessary for me to. I had all my family, everyone one of them. There was never anything between any of us that would make each other unhappy. Strange, they say it never happened but it did. We were always happy and always had a good time together no matter what.

There right in front of me was that road that led this way or that way. I wiped away the tears that trickled from my eyes as I turned to wave goodbye to Dad and Mom standing on the porch. I had a feeling that they were crying just like me. My old dog looked at me and turned around to follow them inside so the good-byes were over.

WELL ON MY WAY TO WHERE

We had no hot water tanks for the home back in those days. In fact I had never heard of an electric hot water heater much less had one in our home. We had no electricity of any kind at our place but we really didn't need any and I presume if we could have had any we would not have wanted it. We loved what we were doing. Maybe it was not the latest thing but it suited the family all right. This was early June, 1927, and the weather was already getting warm so I stopped at a creek down the road and took a good bath. Now I was ready for most anything I might run up on. My hair was somewhat long and shabby as I really did need a haircut. Dad just hadn't taken the time to give me one so now I would have to look further up the road. I would do that some other time if I ever had any. I was way out and I just didn't know how I was going to get back. Should I turn around and go back? Naw man, not just yet, I told myself. Go on man, go on and I'll take care of you no matter what. So I kept on going.

I had not gone but a few miles when I heard a rumbling noise like a wagon coming fast so I kinda waited while I kept on walking slow. I was going down a little grade in the road and the wagon with two horses pulling it appeared over the little rise in the road. The man driving the team hollered out to me to swing on and ride a spell. I need somebody to talk to and youwon't be so tired when you get where you are going to boot. I've been to town and going back home. Have you been walking far? The man asked. Since early this morning I said as I asked for a drink of water from the jug which hung on the back of the seat where the man was driving. Help yourself son. Have you eaten lately. I said that I had two buttered biscuits earlier. Well there's crackers and cheese in the basket right there, help yourself, if you care for some. I thought they were mighty good. Would you mind sir, I asked. He said that if he had minded he wouldn't have told me to eat. Of course I got a cracker and a slice of cheese and crawled up on the seat beside him. We talked and talked some more until he pulled off to go toward his house. Whoa he called to horses as they came to a stop. I guess we'll have to leave now as I am going this way and I think you are going the other way. No one lives out on this road but me. Yes sir I answered. He already knew that I was on my own, so I guess he had no room for me. I crawled off the wagon and started down the road. I waved goodbye and thanked him for the ride. As I turned around for the last look the man said, hey son, take these crackers and cheese as you might get hungry through the night. I thanked him and started on my way. With a few crackers and a hunk of cheese. Boy I was rich and that was all I had. I had eaten my biscuits and butter and some of my crackers and cheese and still had more. The night was coming fast and I didn't know just what I was going to do.

I eased out in a patch of woods for some fifty feet and found a good place to make camp, although I didn't have anything to build a camp with, just what I could get from nature. Ah but that is enough if you know what to do with what nature offers you. I gathered twigs and a log of broken limbs. Scraped out a place where the file would not spread and started a good fire. The weather was wonderful well. A little cook but the fire was warm so I settled down for the night. I sat there for a long spell just gazing into the fire. I began to get lonesome so I took out my ten cent harp and began to play some of the old songs of those days. I played on and on. Finally I fell asleep without realizing it and the night passed without a thought.

The sun was creeping over the hill when I awoke. I rolled myself a Bull Durham cigarette and puffed it slowly and peacefully. After I had eaten the rest of my cheese and crackers I was on my way. The land was getting somewhat flat and the road that was running into the road that I was traveling seemed to be a much more traveled road than the one that I was traveling. Although there were no paved roads in those days, every small town had dirt roads. Some large towns might have had concrete roads but not all that many in this section of the state. I headed north, as good as way as any, I told myself. I walked and walked. No houses were in sight yet. I had walked about eight miles further when I noticed the land was fenced in with barbed wire on the bottom and then heavy hog wire.

On top there was still more heavy barbed wire. This told me that this was a place where swine was raised but this big place. Man there must be a lot of swine in this territory. I was astonished when the barbed wire changed into board fence about six feet high and paintedwhite. All fresh and clean. I just did not know about all of this but maybe I would find out. Out some five hundred yards was a huge white two story house with twelve rooms. A large porch with huge posts or columns I guess I should say. In front was a widows walk above the front door which I would say is the most exciting part of the house. The ceilings were twelve feet high. The huge rooms were filled with the most beautiful antiques I have ever seen. I know it is early to explain how the house looked but I just had to say something about it now. It was lovely. I could heard the soft sound of the big motor that pulled the generator that made the electricity for the lights allover the place. The huge barn, the chicken houses, the big bunkhouse, the mess hall and electric equipment.

The night had begun to color the sky with a blue haze in which a red sun set. Lights where everywhere, looking like a small town off in the distance. Near the house I could hear a thousand loud grunts with squeals in between. All those grunts would tell anyone was that this was a place where hogs were raised. A far off low coming from a lonely cow let me know that there were cows in this place also.

I was afraid but I felt like this was it. If I couldn't get a job here, there wasn't a chance for me. I gently opened the gate, whistling a tune of some song. I don't remember what exactly but when one is afraid, whistling is good for the ego. I carefully walked up to the door and rang the door bell. Three of the biggest dogs I have ever seen met me as I turned around. They looked at me and softly growled. The did not attack me because they knew I loved animals. They sniffed and walked away. When the bell rang on the inside, I heard a voice say, "Hurry James and hold those dogs because they will kill who ever is out there." A well dressed butler quickly opened the door and cried, "In here man, those dogs will eat you alive." I answered, "Oh no sir, they won't bother me, I love dogs and animals always know." Then a tall middle-aged man dressed for dinner walked out and said, "What's going on out here?" The butler quickly answered and said, "This young man, he says the dogs won't bother him." "Boy," the tall man said, "you must be lucky. What are you doing here?" I said, "My name is Billy Jo, Sr. I thought I might get a job with you." He asked, "What can you handle?" I quickly said, "Anything on the farm, sir."

He laughed and said, "This is not a regular farm, boy, this is a hog ranch." I said, "Yes sir, I can handle hogs, cows horses, chickens and dogs." He said," Yes I can see what you did with the dogs, son. Do you know if you have been just about anybody else, your body would have scattered all over this yard?" I nodded and said, "Yes sir." He gestured to the butler, "Get Frenchie to come here. My name is Whit More. What did you say your name was?" I answered again, "Billy Joe Benford, sir." About that time one of the biggest men I have ever seen came walking through the door. Mr. More said, "This is Frenchie, he will take you to the bunk house and chowhall. I'll see you in the morning." He turned and walked away. I looked at Frenchie and said, "My name is." Frenchie said, "I don't want to hear your name boy. Come on to the bunkhouse." "Yes sir," I replied. He said gruffly, "Don't say 'yes sir' to me. Don't say anything." Boy oh boy, I shut my mouth. I wouldn't speak until spoken to. Frenchie led me to the bunkhouse, it was filled with cursing and shouting men. They all shut up when we walked in. "Carry on about your business, boys, "Frenchie said. "If any of you mess with this boy you'll answer to me. Get it? Get it?" Frenchie screamed out. "Come on boy, over in the next building is the mess hall. Some of the boys are still eating. Feed this boy, cook, and keep your mouth shut. Like I just warned the others, if you touch this man, you will report to me. Is that clear?" "Yes sir," they all answered. The first cook sat me down at a table by myself and handed me a well-filled plate. He never spoke a word. He kept his distance and never asked me any questions. I did not understand them but I learned very fast.

The next morning I was taken to the house and the office. The boss, Mr. Whit More was waiting to talk to me. He offered me a job helping on the farm. I called it a swine ranch, but he didn't seem to like that expression so from then on I referred to it as a swine farm. My job was to help with the hogs. I was to help feed the hogs, keep the pens clean and do anything else I was told to do. The pay was real good. I got one dollar a day. When I worked all week I would get seven and one-half dollars. That did not include lodging and three square meals a day. That was real good money.

I never had to go into town as everything I needed or wanted could be bought there at the little store on the farm. It was for the people who worked there on the farm. I guess you could call it a company store. It was handy whatever you wanted to call it. I was very proud. I had only been gone one day and already had a job making more money than I could imagine. Dad and Mom would be proud of me.

While Mr. Whit More was talking I was looking at all the beautiful things that was in the house. Everything was so clean and inviting, I just had to tell about what I saw the first time I entered the door of that house. Kinda strange but I never saw at that time anybody but Mr. Whit More and the bouncers. Punch, Burke and of course, Frenchie. One just did not ask any questions. So I just let it go like it was.

I walked out of that office whistling and singing and went right to work like I had been there for months. Everybody was friendly and I was glad. The wage hands gave me a hand in everything I tried to do.

Now everything was going well after about six months. The job got easier and I was saving lots of money. 1927 was a hard year, everywhere else money was very short and hard to get hold of. I saw a girl looking out of one of the bedroom windows. I saw her several times and she waved at me once or twice. So I knew there was someone in the house besides the one that I had met. I played dumb and I found out later that the girl was named Debbie. She was sixteen years old and very pretty. One day she waved at me very shyly. I only waved back without looking like I was trying to flirt with her. I watched for her everyday. One morning she threw me a long kiss. I was very, very pleased. Perhaps someday I would get to talk to her. Well the time came quicker than I expected. Debbie came down to the hog pens early one morning. We talked for a long spell and she went back to the big house. Very shortly after Frenchie came and ordered me to the office. He said, "The Boss wants you, boy."   Not thinking, I answered, "Yes sir."   "Boy, I have told you not to address me like that," he screamed at me. I said, "I'm sorry, it won't happen again." He growled, "Shut up and get to the office."   I did not answer anymore, just took off as fast as I could walk. I went into the office smiling but I didn't come out smiling. "Billy Joe," the Boss said, "I was looking out of this window just a few minutes ago and you know what I saw? I saw a man talking to my daughter. Do you have any idea who that man was?" Oh yes sir," I said, "it was me. Debbie came down to see me." He said, "Oh, she did. And you have already learned her name?" "Yes sir," I said with my head hanging so low I could see the floor. I knew what was coming. The Boss said, "Billy Joe, I don't want this to happen again."   I said, "Yes sir, I promise. "I promised him faithfully that it wouldn't happen again. But you could guess what happened. Sure enough she would come back to talk to me again. Here comes Frenchie again saying, "Let's go, boy." I knew, yes I knew I had played the devil. In I went. The Boss was looking out of the window again. "Frenchie," he said. "Yes Boss," answered Frenchie. The Boss said, "Teach Billy Joe how to take orders." Frenchie said, "Yes sir, I sure will." The Boss then said, "No, Frenchie, right here, I want to see this." I didn't understand what they were talking about but I soon found out. Frenchie slapped me flat on my back and kicked me with his dirty foot in my mouth. He almost smashed my teeth out. The Boss said, "Frenchie, that's enough. Now boy, do you understand?" I tried to say, "Yes I do," but not much came out. The Boss then said, "Now go back to work." I left hurting and never wanted to see that girl again. But that was not the end of the matter.

About six weeks later, I had to haul off some hog mud, that's what they called the scrapings from the hog pens, when here comes Debbie. She hopped up on the back of the old model T Ford pickup truck. She want with me to the place where we dumped the garbage and so forth. When I got back to the shelter where we kept the truck, there was Frenchie. Oh boy, I knew what was coming. As I walked into the office, the two bodyguards and Frenchie were smiling and rubbing their fists together. Oh boy. The Boss said, "Don't break any bones or do anything that will disturb his work. He's all yours." I was all theirs all right. They slapped me, pinched me, kicked me. Oh man alive. Those three men had them a good workout for the better part of an hour. It seemed like a week. I heard the Boss say, "All right boys, the playing is over, throw him out and go back to work." I dragged myself to the bunkhouse and laid down on my cot. I stayed there for two days and nights with no food or water. The third day I went to breakfast. Everyone laughed and made fun of the way I looked. I was embarrassed to death. I knew I would have to eat or die so I ate. I left the mess hall and went back to work. Things went well. The Boss must have gotten on to Debbie to because she did not show up for a long time. Then I saw her by the window and she threw me a long kiss. I thought maybe she was in love with me. Maybe one day the Boss would let me court her and maybe marry her if I did well and saved my money. One day the Boss sent Frenchie after me to come to the office. Although Frenchie did not go back to the office with me, I want on into the office. The two bodyguards were there but they did not open their months. "Sit down. Billy Joe," the Boss ordered me. I sat down and wondered. "Do you know what you are in here for now. Billy Joe?" the Boss asked. "No sir, what have I done now?" I wondered. The Boss lit a long cigar and said, "Billy Joe, you have given me more service than anyone I have had working here on the farm. I am going to give you a ten dollar bonus and three days off from work. Now you can go into town and spend that hard earned money or just stay here where you can eat, sleep and enjoy fishing down on the lake. Here's your bonus money. I'll see you in two or three days. Have a good time and do what you please."   I thought about asking the Boss if I could see Debbie but changed my mind. So I thought I would do what the Boss had suggested and went back to the bunk-house. I would settle down for the time the Boss had given me.

ALL HELL BROKE LOOSE

As I opened the bunkhouse door, humming a love song of some kind, I was smiling as I walked back to my bunk for a cigarette. I heard that noise that has stayed with me all my life, well I'll say the rest of my life. I looked at my bunk and there lay Frenchie, naked and making love to Debbie who was also naked. My hair stood upon my head. My heart and soul fell like a rock to the bottom and till this day has never been the same. I opened my mouth with a loud curse, "Frenchie, what the hell?" Debbie looked at me and just smiled as she kept the movement in rhythm with her lover. The muscles on Frenchie's body were unbelievable, about two hundred and ninety-five pounds and all man. I bounced my fist off his kidney area on each side and he only gasped for breath. Debbie pushed Frenchie aside and came toward me screaming out, "Oh Billy Joe, Frenchie was raping me, help me, help me."   She was coming toward me with outstretched arms. I waiting until she was in arm's length of me. I felt of my fist, held tight with my left hand. I was crazed by the activities which had happened right before my eyes. I thought she was in love with me. I drew my arm back as far as I could and let go of my fist, striking her right between the eyes. Down she went, out as cold as a cucumber. She was bleeding out of her nose and mouth. I pulled her out of the way, pushed Frenchie off the cot, got him by the leg and pulled him to the center of the bunkhouse. He rolled over and got to his feet. I kicked him in his stomach, another time in the groin. I hit him in the eye with my fist, turned his head and hit him in the other eye. I beat him in the fact till his lips were swelled fit to burst open. With the bottom of my shoe I kicked him under the chin. He still did not go down. I would not get too close to him because if he got his hands on me he would squeeze the life out of me. I think I was praying all the while for God to stop me from my wicked actions then I would think back when he was beating me so. I looked almost as bad as he did afterwards Icould not move for days. Wrestling back then there was no such thing as far as I knew but I had just changed the actions of sports. Walking behind him, I laid him across my back and tried to break his back. I had handled hogs much bigger than Frenchie so it was not hard to do. That move did not faze him. He was still trying to get to his feet. I kicked the biceps on his arms with the toe of my shoe on both arms, then sent to the forearms. Did the same thing to his thigh and calves of his legs. I rolled him over and beat him on his back and rumpus till I had enough of punishment to such a slob. After I smashed his nose flat, I rolled him back over and tried to tear both of his ears off. He lay with both eyes shut, bleeding like a stuck hog so as to say. I walked by Debbie, kicked her as hard as I could, rolled her over to where Frenchie was, pulled her over on top of him and walked out. I went straight to the house where the Boss was in his office, slammed the door open, walked up to his desk and stared him in the face. His two bodyguards only stood there like they were statues. "Boy," Mr. Whit More asked, "What the hell is the matter with you? Where is Frenchie?" "Boss," I said, "Frenchie won't be helping you for some time now. He and your precious little daughter are down in the bunkhouse naked and beaten to hell. I don't know if they will be all right or not and frankly I don't care. Mr. White M ore, I'm going to make this house a hog pen. I'm going to have hogs and picks and every kind of animal in all twelve rooms. I'm not threatening you; I'm making you a promise." He called to his bodyguards, "Punch, Burke, throw him off the porch then go out to the bunkhouse." "Oh Boss, that's all right, I'll just jump if it's all right with you," I said. He snarled, "Get the hell out of here and if there is anything wrong in the bunkhouse, I'll hunt you down like a mad dog." I asked, "And do what Boss? Without Frenchie, you are not worth a damn. I'll be back real soon Boss." I climbed up onto the banister and jumped to my feet on the ground. I thought as I was going down. Lord, I'll be torn to pieces when I hit the ground. But I was hardly shaken. Lucky I suppose but I didn't care if the two men had killed me. I don't think I would have moved a hand to protect myself. I was so deeply hurt, knowing it was all over with Debbie and me. I left the yard, hit the road and started toward home sweet home.

HOME SWEET HOME

I'll never forget that free feeling that I had when I left that driveway and left that farm. I stepped out into the road belonging to the county and I was included in that county. I walked proudly toward home I really expected Punk and Burke, the two bodyguards, to catch up with me and take me back and perhaps kill me. I just couldn't make myself run and hide from anybody anymore. I realized that I didn't have to have the biggest biceps in the world to get by. Just hold your own, that's all it takes.

About dusk I reached the place where I had spent my first night alone when I left home. I just looked at the place, smiled and kept on walking. Sometime later on that night I heard the creaking of the planks that made the bridge. As I passed the little clump of trees I looked toward the house and saw the little light was still burning in the window. Home sweet home. I felt that lump in my pocket, the sack with all the money I had saved in it. I felt like taking it out and scattering it allover the place. Then I thought, how am I going to prove to Mom and Dad that I had been working. I just held on to it. Sooner or later I would have to take it out and I would have it ready.

My good old dog raised his head, shook himself and stretched as if to say, "Billy Joe, come on in."   he acted like I had only been gone for a few hours, but I think he was proud to see me. Mom and Dad were already up and at whatever they did. They always got up early in the mornings, why I'll never know. I guess you set yourself to a tradition then you keep it up. I smelled the scent of meat and eggs cooking when I walked up on the porch. Dad hollered out, sounding frightened, "Whose there?" I said, "Me, Dad, Billy Joe, cane I come in?"   I was smiling. I heard Mom say in a low voice, "It's Billy Joe, open the door Pa, hurry." They both came to the door. They were already dressed and I really could smell that odor again. Fat back and scrambled eggs cooked on a wood stove. Everything smells different if it is cooked on a wood stove. Mom cried, "Lord have mercy, come on in here boy. Give me a big old hug." Dad shut the door as Mom led us into the kitchen where she had been cooking. She said, "Sit down boy in your old place and dig in." We held hands while Dad said Grace and gave thanks for the return of his son. Then we dug in. I just believe we talked the rest of the night. That was all right. I was proud to get back home. Mom even told of the plans they had made for when they passed away. I made her change the subject but she gave me the will. After all I had seen back at the big house, money and lots of land was no big deal to me. Everything had been left to me. Over six hundred acres of land even though at the time about three hundred dollars was the most we could have gotten for the whole lot. But you know that was a lot of money back then but the fact was I didn't want it anyway and I intended to take care of them as long as they lied or as long as I lived anyway. Nothing had changed at that time so we just talked on, ate and talked some more.

SATISFACTION DOES NOT MAKE IT RIGHT

When Mom and Dad passed away there was nothing left for me out there so I immediately went to town. I took care of all the business and found a place to live then went on for there. I was all alone in the world. Although I had brothers and sisters, I hardly ever saw them. They did not want any of the money or anything from the old place. Too many memories. We all had a good childhood and many happy memories, so must let it be like it is. I had stayed at home and taken care of Mom and Dad until I was sixteen years old and they had wanted me to get out on my own while they were well and could take care of themselves. I know the last two and a half years I wasn't much help but I could always be found if they needed me. There in town I worked wherever I could find work. Maybe not what I wanted, but a job where I could pay my room rent and eat well. That was good enough for me. I know I was and still am tight when it comes to spending money but I don't mind not spending everything I can get hold of just to be doing something. I only had a few dollars that I had saved when Dad and Mom died. I still had the money that I got from the home place. That was very smart because when the right time came it helped me do what I had planned in my mind all the time. I always knew that I would do just what I said.

THE BEGINNING OF THE END

I always got a newspaper every morning. I loved the funnies and especially the brown section in the Sundays issue. I liked to read Flash Gor-
don in the funnies. But as you know everything turned out to be kinda
true to life in the things that was written in that issue. I was never interested in politics or government issues. This special morning the first thing
that struck my eye was exciting. I read it, ran to the place where I was
working and got off for the day. The people needed me very much where
I worked but that didn't matter with me. I read the article over and over.
I trembled and shook so back it frightened me. After I settled down and
came to my senses I found out for sure. The article read, "The hog farm
of Mr. Whit More was for sale. If interested get in touch with the owner
immediately."   I knew that I had better not try to approach the farm
myself. So I got the best lawyer I could find to check into it for me that
very day. We talked about the price that it might be worth and what I
could afford to pay. We agreed on everything. I let him know that, that
place was mine and if he was interested in it he could have it after I had
finished with it. No funny stuff, no crooked dealing, just plain business.
If he could not handle it, then he had better tell me so. This tome was
serious business and I wanted that farm. OK? "Okay," the lawyer said,
"We'll get it at any cost but as cheap as possible. I'll start now."   I told
him, "Yes sir, that's what I want. Bring me the deed because I've got the
cash."

About three o'clock, a knock at the door had me looking for the caller.
It was the lawyer, all smiles. I got it. I got it. He was so proud that he
could take care of my business so well and he let me know it. The price
was right and the deal was closed. We were to pick up the deed at five

o'clock at my office. He continued to smile. At five o'clock, Mr. White Moore came by the office with Punk and Burke, the two bodyguards. I had told the lawyer to tell me when the deal was done. I was waiting in the back room. He told me when they were finished and I have never seen a more surprised man in my life, when I walked out of that room. Mr. Whit Moore couldn't speak. Punk and Burke put their hands on their guns but Mr. Whit Moore stopped them. "This man is only carrying out his promise, let him alone," he said. Punk broke in with "Yes Boss but Frenchie?" Mr. White Moore broke in, "If you ever mention that name to me again, I'll personally kill the both of you. Is that clear?" They both answered, "Yes sir." Mr. Whit Moore looked at me and said, "We are going home now to pack. We'll be out by morning boy." He walked away. You know I wish I had given that farm back to him and let it go as my personal loss. I was young then as far as getting even I think the argument that very moment I walked out into view, he knew that I had fulfilled my promise and there was nothing else to do.

I thought maybe they would burn the house down that night but when I got there the next morning it was just like it was the last time I saw it. Some of the men were still there. Although the hogs were squealing for food, the hands did not seem to know what to do. I told them to bring what food was left and scatter it though the house. I told them to put it in every room throughout the house upstairs and downstairs. Then turn the hogs loose in the house. Lead them in her with the food, they will come as they are starving. I looked around in the house at some of the nicest antiques I have ever seen. Everything was clean as a pin, shinning like a diamond. On the bed in Debbie's room lay a beautiful night gown. Although it had just come off her pretty back, my heart fell to my stomach as I remembered that morning when her and Frenchie were having that affair in the bunkhouse. Oh God, why did I have to remember that? By the time I had finished with my prayer, asking God to forgive me for what I was doing, hogs were covering every room in the house. The men had poured feed everywhere. Hogs were coming up the stairs like they owned the place. They were never penned up again. I walked out of the house where the curtains were blowing out of the windows. The men were going their way and me? Well I walked back to town, broke as a ghost, crying like a baby and whistling all at the same time. It was over and again. God forgive me.

Where Daydream And Fantasy Meet

Where Daydream And Fantasy Meet

"Lesia, Madge", Git yore lazy bones out a that air bed and cleanup this hare house. Seems like youns dont never git notin done no mo.

Yes mama, wees coming. Mama, don't wens have notin to eat nomo?

"No, Wens don't have notin to eat" Maby yore Pa. Will bring home sometin, whence never he comes in.

He had bed not brang home notin to eat, unless hims got me sometin to drank. "You youngons knows I got to have my boose, ifins youns dont never eat. "Does youns here me? Youns dont eat tills I drank.

Thems thar ain't no doctors odors, thems thar is my orders. Does youns understand?

Yes Mama, wens understand.

The youngest girl Lesia, said to Madge, whut does understand mean Madge?

It means, well, like doe youns knows whut I said.

Madge was six years old and Lesia was only five years old. They never went to school. They new of nothing that went on out side of their house or yard, where they lived, behind a big red hill with their father an mother. Billy Bob Welch and his wife Ruby.

Billy Bob, tried to work to feed his family. Work was hard to find, but Ruby was addicted to hard drinking, so to keep piece and safety for his children. Billy Bob tried his best to please Ruby and keep her supplied with drink. Ruby always found some reason to beat the girls, and Billy Bob was afraid of Ruby. He was in a no win situation.

When Ruby was in her bed, in a drunk sleep, the girls would goin to the woods that was near by, through the bushes they would wonder, picking berries, finding nuts and any thing to eat to stay a live, they very seldom had a good meal.

The days that Bill Bob was able to get something to cook , he would wait until Ruby was a sleep to cook so he and the girls could eat. He was careful to put something aside for Ruby. As the saying goes. Ruby ate like a hog.

Ruby was so far gone from the effects of her drinking, she could only think of her next drink.

There were no neighbors any where around, the family being isolated, they lived every day, like the day before. Trying to stay out of Ruby's sight, and waiting for Billy Bob to retum. home.

Billy Bob had worked around a mans house, as he was dumping trash he found some clothes that would fit the girls. Some sweaters and blouses that they were proud to get. The work did not last very long, but Billy Bob could never bring his self to discuss his family to any one. There might have been plenty of things that the family could have used, but Billy Bob thought asking some body for something was low rating the people that he was suppose to take care off, so he kept on trying.

There was fear in the house hold along with hunger. The girls were loved by their father but he showed no affection toward them. He encouraged no affection for hin from the girls, afraid of the half crazed Ruby.

One night when the girls were in bed, snuggling close, Madge begin to whisper to Lesia. " Lesia, Wes gotta git away from here befons wens starves to death. When Pa brings in food again, wens will put someufit away. When wens have saved some food, wens will git going. Lesia does youns wants to do this?? " Uh hu, Lesia sniffled. "Do you think Pa will care"? But we have no choice, Madge replied. I think Pa will understand. He knows that she beats us., that wens air hungry. Maybe wens willbe better off. " Can youns go with me Lesia" "Uhhu I will go." she said. Then turned over and they both went to sleep.

The next morning. Ruby awoke with a long git outa bed you two, and c lean up this nasty shack. Hear Me? Git up.

Lesia and Madge jumped out of their bed and ran to where their mother lay in her bed.

"Madge " Ruby screamed, bring my bottle" now, hurry up.

Yes Mama, Madge said, her hands trembling with hunger and fear. Almost throwing as she carried the uncapped bottle, the odor was so strong hitting her in the nose. Billy Bob had already left looking for a days work. He was as hungry as the girls, but he always saw that they had food before he ate anything.

Billy Bob, passed by an old griss mill a few miles from where theylived. He noticed that flower was every where even on the window seals. Hurrying over to the flower that some one had spilled, he began eating hands fall like it was cake of some kind. The miller saw him, he called out "Man what are you doing"?" "Mister" Billy Boy replied, I am hungry, please let me have the flower on the window seal. No man , in here. Take my breakfast food, eat it all and there's coffee over on the stove help yourSelf. "No," Billy Bob" told the miller no. Then he told him about his two girls with out food. How can I eat when I know that they are hungry.

Where are the girls? The miller asked. Billy Bob told him that he was out every day looking for work, but could find one or two days a week. Some days not even one day. The miller gave him a sack of flour, and a sack with two dozen eggs in it. There was meat in the meat boxeso he gave him some meat. Here take this home with you and feed your family.

Billy Bob lost no time getting home he hurried in the house, put the food on the table, went straight to the wood pile for stove wood to cook the food with. As he started back in to the house. Ruby was standing in the door with the food in her hands. Git this stuff outa here if youins don't I will throw it out in the yard. Billy Bob droped the wood and grabbed the food. No you don't Ruby, not this time or ever again you are through.

Where is my bottle? You aint got none. Ruby, you will never have any more if I have to bring it to you. "Git outa my way Ruby, move for the last time.

Billy Bobb and Ruby were yelling back and forth. Ruby looking like a sick witch with no where to go.

"Oh God" Billy Bob said, as he started toward the stove, with the wood that he picked up off the floor, at least I saved the food.

Madge and Lesia was in the comer of the kitchen holding on to each other nervously whispered.

Billy Bob started the fire and begin making biscuits. Oh they smelt so good and that fat back "oh yeah" He fried some fat back cooked some eggs and made grave and plenty of it too.

Ruby joined in and ate as much as any body.

Every time Ruby tried to speak Billy Bob shut her up. Don't say nothing Ruby don't even speak. When you get full we got some talking to do. Ruby in a loud tone of voice , bellowed out at Billy Bob. Now what did you want to talk about? Yes Ruby, I want to talk about you. Ruby, you.

I know you don't got no learning like me but you do know what you're doing wrong.

I aint doing notin wrong Billy Bob, you just don't know whut Ims going through. Them two youngens Billy Bob is driving me crazy.

 Ruby shut your mouth them are my two girls. Don't you talk like that you're still drunk. Well you had better git sober now or Im gona get you sober. Ruby if I ever know you done some thing wrong or something you autin to either of them air chilen, I'll hurt you bad Ruby, hear me? Yes I hear you Billy Bob. But I ain't listening to you Billy Bob. Hear Me?

Lesia, and Madge, were hid under the table over by the window, where no one could see them.

That talk only fortified the things that they had planed to do.

Lesia, and Madge, once more, got to together on their plans. They were worried thinking their Pa. Would not bring Ruby another bottleif not they would have to change their plans.

As Billy Bob was leaving, in the morning, to go look for work, Ruby went to the edge of the porch and softly reminded Billy Bob to bring her a bottle of. You know what., and I will have you something good to eat when you git home . Now I wonder what that would be. He said to himself.

Billy Bob only turned and looked at Ruby, and walked away.

Ruby only turned and walked back into the house, she seemed to be very happy, thinking that Billy Bob would bring her some whisky back.

Lesia, and Madge. Listened while Ruby tried to hum as she pretended to work.

Every thing went well for a few minutes, until Billy Bob got out hearing distance, then it broke loose again. This time Ruby screamed out at the girls. Both of you youngons git hare, I got work for you to do.

Slapping each of the girls on the cheek very, pushed them out of the door screamed out loud as she could, go pick me some poke salad and git back hare.. Yore daddy wants some fer supper and iffins you all wants to eat you best git some fer several days, cause thats all wensgot and wens aint got that yet. Don't come back hair wit out some ether.

Lesia said to Madge ifins wens had our bread, now would be a good time to jis keep on a going. Sho would , Madge said to Lesia, but we ns ain.t got none yit, but maby soon. \

The girls hunted all day for some poke salad, but never found any. Tired and half starved, they started home

Looking across the field, they saw Billy Bob going down the road toward home.

They ran and caught their Daddy. They were very proud knowing that he would protect them from their mother.

What are you two girls doing out here by your selves?

Wens are looking fer Poke salad, but thay aint none. No Billy Bob said, not this time of year. If you hada fount some, it would have been blooming and berrying and it would have been poison to eat.

Pa youd better tell Ma about that, cause ifens wens hada fount any Ma woulder cooket it and we woulder all been dead by morning .

I will tell ser girls , I will tell her. She want be cooking no mo poke salad this year.

Whetcha you got under yore arm Pa, Ma a bottle? You just nevermind whut I got under ma arm, you tend to yore own business.

Yeah, Pa, Madge said in a low voice and they scampered on down the road toward home.

Madge and Lesia, got their things to gather, all the clothes they had, all the matches they could find, an old pot, a small biscuit pan, They put it behind a tree, including some fish hooks an two short cane poles they could use for fishing poles.

When Ruby got drunk again and went to sleep, they would be long gone.

Time passed Ruby walked around like she was in heaven, so to say.

Seems as though, things were changing but no not yet. Ruby was sipping a little ever few minutes.

Dinner was approaching fast and Ruby was still going strong .She called the girls for dinner. Lesia, and Madge came into the kitchen half scared to death. Knowing if they showed any guilt. Ruby would spot it in a second. So they had to be very careful.

Billy Bob had managed to get a days work some where so he had bough some beans milk and unions, that was what they had for supper.

Girls this is good. Right?

Yes Mama they both agreed. Thanks for the good dinner. Mama. Any thing to eat would have been good, as hungry as they were. This was the first time Ruby had cooked in quiet some times. It would have to be very bad for those two to say any thing unless they were agreeing with Ruby.

The girls Madge and Lesuia, were trying to be very nice so Ruby would not suspect any thing this was going to happen just as soon as Ruby got drunk and went to sleep. So they waited and watched, being as quiet as possible.

Soon it happened. Ruby took out her bottle which was in the cabinet under the kitchen sink, took a big snort and held her breath for few second then let go, saying whew that was good.

Shortly after that she took another and another. Until she could hardly walk to the bed., where she was preparing for a long nap. She took one more good drink and fell across the bed, snoring and snorting, went to sleep. The girls eased into their bedroom, watched every move that took place. Madge noticed Ruby noticed the stopper was off the bottle, so she walked over to where the bottle was and pushed the stopper down. She knew if Ruby picked up the bottle that the whiskey would probably run out all over the bed and she would not get drunk.

Both Lesia and Madge ran out of the house, grabbed their things which they had gotten ready for their trip into the unknown and started running across the field., not knowing or caring where they were going. They ran to the nearest body of woods they could find. Trying not to make any tracks so they could not be followed.

Hey did not want to be found. They wanted to get as far away as possible, as quick as possible.

They found a small branch of water as they went along .Their loads were heavy and they were getting tired. Madge threw her load down and told lesia to do the same. Lesia did as Madge told her and they Settled down for a while. Just a few minutes of rest was all they were going to do. This place was quiet, no one around, so they fell asleep.

It was almost dark when they awoke. Madge shook Lesia and told her that it was getting dark. The place where they lay down to rest was awas a nice place to make camp and spend the night. Preparing for supper was wasn't to hard. Madge had gotten up the scraps that was left over at their last meal, so they had scraps and branch water for supper.

What A Night

The night was the worst night the girls had ever spent. It was so dark they could not see anything. No light, no moon, no nothing. Lesia begin to sniffle and cry. She was afraid, in fact she was scared to death.

After about two hours in the darkness, they decided to build a fire. Madge had brought the matches and there were plenty of twigs, small limbs, and plenty of dry straw to start the blaze. Crawling around on the grown they gathered sticks and straw, in a few minutes they had a good fire going. The girls were not afraid nearly so much. Madge waited for Lesia to go to sleep then she dozed of and did not wake up until the morning when the sun was shining in their eyes. The night went over and the girls were rested. Again they gathered more sticks and large limbs, made the fire hot enough to cook breakfast. Madge made some biscuits out of the flour they had brought with them. The spring branch water was as cold as ice and it was used to put in the biscuits. Madge had put in two eggs that Billy Bob had brought from the mill that gave him the flour. Of course they did not have any grease to go in the food but the eggs turned out well they ate them with out noticing any thing wrong.

Breakfast was finished , they packed up and started on their way .Lesia talked about how good the breakfast was, that made Madge feel Better to know she was taking the trip well. Any thing would be better than what they had at home, because their mother could not cook. Billy bob cooked most of the time, and his food was not all that good. The only reason they ate, was because they had no choice. Billy Bob usually went to work with out breakfast, and must have eaten before he came home, but they made out some how.

Lesia and Madge, put out the fire and poured water on the coals to make sure the fire would not catch up again. After they were sure the fire was out, they covered up their camp sight with plenty of straw and sticks, no one could ever tell that they had been there, just in case someone came looking for them.

They washed the dishes, and was on their way again. They had gone a long way, the land was hilly, so they stayed near the stream, the water was good and cold, and there it was , any time they wanted it.

Lesia, was walking near the stream, where it was flowing over rocks, a good place to play, all of a sudden she called out to Madge. "Madge, she said, come down here, look over there next to the bank, a fish.

Yeah, I see him. There's, She ran back to where she had laid the supplies, got two little cane poles and gave one to Lesia.

Madge showed Lesia how to put a hook on the line and attach it to the pole. Hurriedly they got out and scratched in the leaves and found some worms. Quickly they started fishing.

These two girls didn't have a worry in the world, just having a good time. So they fished own and on.

Lesia caugh a large horn head, so did Madge. After they had caught enough for supper, They new not to catch more than they could eat, so they found a good place to cook the fish. Madge cleaned the fish and got them ready for the pan, while Lesia found lots of straw and limbs to start and keep the fire going.

The fire got going, Madge stuck the end of the cane pole through the fish and gave to Lesia. Turning the fish over and over while they cooked was lots offim. Madge had done it before, with Billy Bob, Her father when they some times went fishing. Bread that was saved from the last meal came in handy. The fish were good, they enjoyed it all.

Both the girls had been fishing while they were very young so they knew how to fish, catch, clean and cook any kind of fish, now it came in handy for the both of them. They knew how to get around to do any thing that they had to do.

After they had finished their meal cleaning up was no job at all. Laying down in a pine grove, near the stream there was plenty of straw to make a bed. Being tired a little rest would take care of what ever.

Madge turned to Lessa, and said.

Lesia, Do, you want to go back home?

"No" Lesia quickly answered.

But wens don't have much to eat.

"Well" wens don't have much to eat at home, and wens aint got beat yet.

"No" I don't I don't want to go back home, any way Ruby would kill usens .

No , Lesia, not Ruby, Mama.

Every thing was quiet, as they went to sleep for a long nap.

Madge awoke and jumped to her feet, she had been dreaming a n awful bad dream. Although she could not remember what it was about, she finely lay down by Lesia and slept a while longer.

About midnight, they awoke and rubbed their eyes.

"Man'" Lesia said, wens must a slept a week.

Madge, I feel better after wens took that air nap.

I does too, Madge said after yawning a long yawn.

The darkness did not seem to bother them at all right now, so they huddled up close and went back to sleep.

Morning came fast and they were ready to go when they awoke.

Lets go on yonder way. Wens gotta find some more food pretty soon now. Wens only got enough bread for another day or two.

Madge, Lesia said, lets catch some more fish tomorrow, I aint hungry right now. And wens can save that air flour.

"Oh" well Madge said so they went on their way.

An hour or so passed, they were walking into a sweet gum orchid every thing was lovely and they were happy.

Madge, suddenly stopped' Look Lesia look , there's usan a tree hut look down near the ground., Lesia.

They both ran over to where the tree was. A huge sweet gum tree which was hollow at the bottom. The walls of the hollow was thin butthe tree was strong. The opening was big enough that the girls could get into it very easy. The inside of the tree was smooth and clean like it had been washed. They stood back to take a peak insuring them selves that there was nothing inside to harm them. It was empty so they inspected and examined it well.

It was a good place to stay and in case a shower they would keep dry. With a brush they flapped down all of the spider webs and swept the floor. It would be a good place to live for a while. Lesia sat down in the hallow and leaned back against the wall of the tree. She put her hands to gather as Madge stepped inside the hole. Being big and high enough that they could move around with out bother. They called it their house' As

Madge looked down at Lesia, Lesia said, with a sad look on her face
Thank youns Jesus for our new home and dozed off to sleep.

The two slept for a long time. They awoke and realized that it was late
Madge checked the flour in the sack in which they carried it all the way
there was still quite a bit left in it. So Madge made up a hoe cake and put
it in the pan.

Lesia was trying to build a fire with some twigs and some straw>Madge
then got up some larger twigs and limbs from a near by tree, and sat
them ready for some hot coals for to cook the bread.

The coals were just right in no time at all. Soon the bread was ready as
soon as it got cold.

Madge looked toward a sound that she knew was a falling limb. That
broke and fell to the ground. Then she saw a large vine of ripe musca-
dines. just ready to eat. They would be good with their bread. She gathered lots of them, and they ate until they were full and lazy.

The sun was going down, but the darkness had not sat in yet, so they
sat around the fire just talking and discussing their thoughts.

Madge, Lesia said Why aint Ma and Pa come looking fer usens? They
dont love usens at all. Do they Madge?

Cose they does Lessa. Youns know they does .Why don't thems wants
usen Lesia asked again.

I don't knows , sis I don't knows. Maby when theys finds usnsliving in
a tree hole theys will want usns then. Theys will feel sorry ferusns and
change thes ways about life and usens..

Lesia and Madge knew very well that they would need someclothes
real soon, and they did not know how they were going to get them. If
there. If there were a store near by, they would be afraid to go in around
people because they might be recognized and put in a home some where,
or in a place where they would not be free to do any thing they wanted to
do. No sir they had had enough of that already.

The nights were cool, and the stream did not help the matter any. The
moisture made it worse. The girls got some large limbs and sticks, lots of
them and put them around in front of the tree, where they could easily
get to them if the night got any colder. They pushed the hot coals nearer
to the hole in the tree in good reach now the limbs could be put on the
fire very easily .

After they had talked a while and Madge tried to teach Lesia a few words that she had learned and how they might be spelled. Although Madge had only gone to school a short time so she had not learned very much she knew every little thing would. Finely they both went to sleep. Morning came early, Madge fixed a small breakfast, just a little Cake of bread was all they could afford. They tried to stretch what they had.

After a while the girls got their fishing poles and started fishing. Catching several nice size cat fish, making them very happy. Lesia tried to help get the fish ready for cooking. Madge, got water in the little pan, getting sand from the stream rubbed the fish until all the slime was gone.

When they were having fun, time passed quickly, Deboning the fish cutting all the uneatable parts away, they began cooking the them. There had no grease to cook the fish in, so they had to leave the skin on. Laying them on the hot coals. Soon there was a dinner that you wouldn't believe. Good and hot, and enough for a feast. Eating all they wanted and took a nap. This was heaven to them, two little girls that did not know what was coming next.

The girls caught several bull frogs and ate their legs, good cooked on hot coals, just a little salt was all it took. Once they caught a large turtle finding it hard to get apart, finely cut off the legs and had a feast. Anything eatable to stay alive.

Danger Lurked

One morning the girls were awaken by the awful noise of dogs barking .Lots of them, dozens, of them. Dogs were everywhere barking howling, growling, there were all kind of dogs, any kind one might think of. Large ones, small ones, any color. Some were pretty, some were ugly. They all seem to be vicious.

What's going on, Madge, Lesia asked raising up on her elbows?

"Oh" just a bunch of dogs, just looking fer fun, I guess.

I'm scared, said Lesia, with a frightful look in her eyes and a trimmer in her voice. I don't like dogs, shu them away, Madge.

Theys a bunch or wild dogs, Lesia, and wen's dont want to disturb thems, theys might git usn. Youns knows? So just be quiet and maby thems will go away.

Several dogs would come to the door at a time. Snapping and growling, and snapping like they were going to eat the girls alive.

Madge crawled to the edge of the opening, grabbed the limb that she used to pull the coals closer to the opening when they got cold, and jabbed at the dogs. One was stuck good so he screamed and ran off and did not return. Dogs were all around just waiting for the attack.

Right in front of the door, stood a huge shepherd with his fangs showing looking in. As he lifted his lips to growl, he seemed to recognize Madge., and he quieted down, as did the rest of the pack. One small black and tan dog though he would come on in any way. The shepherd growled at him again, but the little dog continued to bark and growl. The shepherd caught him by the neck and slung him back and forth several times. When the shepherd turned him loose, he just lay there and whined. Crawling up to the hole, lay there and whined.

The pack seemed to take heed to what happened, they all lay down so there was quietness from then own.

Madge, scared half to death. Tied her shoe laces and went out side the tree house, to cook breakfast. Not even one dog howled or growled she made up what bread that was left and started the fire

When each of the dogs got warm, they only crawled off. The shepherd lay there like he was guarding the place and watching Madge and lesia. After the bread was done, the girls ate what they wanted then gave the scraps to shep. Shep was what they together named the dog. He seemed to thank them by licking their hands. Crawling on all four legs to where they sat drinking water, Lesia offered the dog some water, he licked the cup, struck his tung into the cup to get more.

Staying there for a good long while, the dogs finally got up and took off down by the stream, but the shepherd just lay there. In a little, while the girls cleaned up what dishes and pans they had, they crawled back into their tree hut and talked about what they had to do. They knew that they were out of food and would be getting hungry very soon..

Lessa and Madge were growing weary, as they walked along the stream. Their hearts throbbing as they walked. In the middle of the day, they though maby they would catch another fish, since they were getting hungry, so they did. The dog was still with them. He never came close enough for the girls to tough him, but he was there and they loved it.

They cough several fish when the meal was over, Lesia gave the dog the scraps again he licked her hand when he was finished. While she stroked his back and neck, he was getting us to being with them.

As night approached, they built another fire in a good spot where they could sleep if they got sleepy. The shepherd lay there with them. They felt so much safer with shep around. As they gathered more wood, they noticed where some one had been roaming around. They looked for more signs but never saw any more. Oh well could have been them wild dogs so they said. They lay down on the straw and leaves that they had gathered and went to sleep. The dog crawled up as close as he could get to the girls and lay quiet all night.

The sun was coming up to be another day. All of a sudden, the shepherd got to his feet, looking around showing his fangs and growling. Then it happened, out from behind a huge tree. The most ugliest creature Of a man , they had ever seen. He stood there for a while then hollered out. Whut youns doing on my land ? Stealing my fish and burning my wood ? Chep walked over close with his fangs showing. Stop thatar dog now, or I'll kill him wit this her stick.

Madge spoke to chep just like he was her own dog, down chep lay down. The dog acted just like he knew what she was talking about, he just lay down and kept quiet, watching every move that man made.

I axed you whut you doing on my land? I ant axin you no mo.

Wes lost mister.wens have been lost fer fo days. Wens dont got notin to eat, wens bout to starve, sos wens had to cotch some fish to stay live.

Den whetcha doin wit all thar air stum youns carrying?

Wens wus out hiking, and got lost, mister

Youns air two pretty little ones, whar did youns come from?

Wens dont know wherins wrens come from. Madge answered.. Wens dont know wherenswens come from.

Well I recons Ims gona have to take youn home wit me, til ims can find out wherenceyouns. Come own over here and leave tharair dog hear.

Wens cant wens dont own thatair dog. Hes aint er coming wit unses no hare.

The old man took Madge and Leisa across the stream and headed away from it leaving it far behind.

Over on the side of the hill, in the dense woods, there was an old log cabin built in the side of the hill where no one could see it from any directions.

The old man opened the door and told the girls to git in thatair house.

That place smelt so bad the girls could not stand it.

There was a fire softly burning in the fire place, looked so warm and cozy.

Lesia and Madge lay there things down and sat down on the dirt floor. There was a sheet iron stove with a oven, the pipe ran out the top of the house, looked to have been there for a hundred years.

The old man sat there in his stick back chair and grinned at the girls.

Yall shore air a pretty pair or girls , ya' 11 gons be mine now Ain't you? Lesia and Madge, did not speak. Aincha, I said aincha?

Wens recon wens are Wens don't know.

I does I knows youns air. Youns aint going no where. I benner looking fer some pretty little girls just like youll. Now I's got me some, Ims gona keep youns too.

Lesia and Madge was getting more afraid by the minute. Chep lay quietly on the out side of the house, they felt safe with him around, although he was yet a stranger.

Now you gals git up you done rested enough, and clean this place up. Then cook something good to eat. Cook enough fer all us air youns ainter gona have none.

Whetch youns got to eat? Madge asked the old man .

Youns will find sometin over thar in that air comer, under thatair table, so start cooking.

The girls got up and started cleaning the place. There was spider webs and spiders too.

Roaches, bugs of all kinds, ants every where. You name it, it was there. They swept out the place with a broom sage broom. Inside looked and smelled much better.

Madge found some beans, fresh eggs plenty of fat back, hams hanging from the sealing behind the curtain that covered up the comer of the room. The old man, had chickens, a cow and a large garden. The girls were glad because there was plenty of good food. Butter, flour in the flower jar and lots more in a barrel.

Their supper was good, the old man ate like a pig and so did Madge and Lessa.

Lessa sat at the table with her head berried in her hands as if she was sick.

What's wrong Lesia? Madge asked, as she laid her hand on her back to comfort her. I don't know, Lesia replied, raising her head looking at her sister. The tears were pouring from her eyes. Madge, while we were eating. Did you think of Mama and Papa? Yes I did, Sis, I thought how pa would have eaten if he had some of our food. " Oh Madge, what can we do to repay them for raising us. They had an awful hard time. Pa never had a job, Ma was always drunk , Oh Madge lets go home. Lesia, be quiet, that old man might hear you and start asking questions. Alright Madge, I'll try. Lesia, have you noticed how you talk? You talked like Pa did , not like Ma. What is happening to us? I don't, but I noticed you talking different since we met that old man. I though that was because you heard the way he talked. Well I guess that is one reason, I dont know. Lets try to keep it up. Just don't say any thing about it. We'll see what happens. You know we all might learn something from us meeting each other, Lesia. You can never tell.

The scrape were given to the dog, so every one was full and sleepy.

The table was cleaned up the dishes were done while the old man took a nap. As he slept, he watched them with one eye open so they just let him sleep.

Lesia and Madge talked it over and decided to do what the old man told them to do so he would be proud and et them stay.

He was proud of the girls alright king of his domain and he knew it. He would look at them and sing his little song but they couldn't learn the words to the song.

One day Madge was in the house, the old man was sitting on the out side, and singing his little song. Over and over.

I've been thinking all my life
where I could find my self a wife.
Down in the woods where the grass is green
I found the two prettiest girls I ever seen .

I know just what I'm gona d
raise me a wife like I want too.
I'll teach them how to feed and milk the cow
I'll teach them every thing that they don't know how.

When they are grown if they are pretty and fine.
I'll make both of them little girls mine.

Madge, ran back to where Lesia was sitting holding her hands to her face and shaking.

What's wrong Madge? Lesia asked.

Go listen to that song he's singing, don't let him know you heard him. Go on, Madge insisted.

Lesia eased over and listened. She came running back crying and shaking too Calm down, Lesia calm down. If he sees us crying like this he might hurt us.

Madge was thinking, " What's next." what can I do" she said to her self. I don't know. I'm only six years old and I couldn't know nothing. If I was a only a little older, then what? Would it be the same? Would Lesia be the same? How did all of this come about?

Madge, she said to her self, just hold on there must be better than this some day, so justhold on and see it through. Help Lesia make it the best way any one could. You can do it, you know.

Lesia was getting worried, because the old man laughed all the time. She though maby he planing on eating both of them. But Madge quieted her down telling her since he was laughing that he was pleased and would not hurt them. In fact, Madge believed he was proud to have some one around.

Even after the both of them heard him singing his little song, they wondered what he was talking about.

The old man was always trying to eat. He said that he did not like poor women, he liked fat women, that's why Lesia was afraid he was getting ready for some girl stew. Naw, naw Madge told her, naw nothing like that. Wens are warm at nite an got sometin to eat. So whut wens need to do is to lam every thing wens can rite now.

What kind of talk are you doing now, Madge? You done forgot already.

I did not forget anything I was only thinking of Mama, that's all I knew you would pick that up Lesia.

Lesia, You teach me and I will teach you every thing I know. Lets don't talk like that old man. You know? Yeah Madge I know what you mean Ma and Pa talked like that but Pa had a better learning than Ma did and we want never around Pa much so we just talked like Ma talked.

We are going to find it hard to start talking like Pa did but that old man he talks bad . We never talked like this all the time till we moved here. I know sis but we have been talking better since we started talking and you , just like me have been listening to every word I said to make sure it was right. Well that's what you said you teach me and I will teach you.

When we start to school we want to know something better than we know now.

Madge, Lesia said do you think Ma and Pa ever looks for us? I don't know thats twice you have asked me that I just don't know. Wens dont care ifins they dont. Ma is always drunk and Pa is always trying to find a way to get her something else to drink. Madge, You done messed up some more. I know Lesia I know Lets don't mention Ma and Pa no more. I go back to them every time we mention them. You know Madge they might do better with out us so dont worry any more till we have to.

But I don't care if we never see them again, cause they dont want want us around any way. Well we will get along fine you be proud like me for all this.

"Oh'" I am proud for everything, I think we done just right> We might be sorry some day but right now, were alright

I'm getting big to, Lesia said as she smiled and looked at Madge. "Madge" she said with her mouth wide open. You are getting big too. Look at you. Yes I know Lesia, Madge said with a what's next look in her eyes, as she continued to scratch her fingers.

Do we ever have another birthday like little Billy George did. You know that little boy that lived next to us over yonder did? I don't know, Madge said turning her head from one side to the other looking at her fingers as tho she had never seen them before.

Something has just hit Madge like a ton of brick, she smiled as she hummed an old fashion love song.

You know, Lesia, we are gonna be women some day and the way we are going now, itant going to be long, so we had better start working on our selves rite now.

What are we going to put on our face like Ma did? Sho ain't nothing here, ho Madge?

Lesia was kinda getting worried thinking about that. She wanted to be in shape when they started to school.

What is that stuff over there that the old man puts on his hands when he gets through milking the cow? I don't know , Lesia but I think he called it taller. I think that's what he said.

Well, if that's what he called and it's good enough for him, its good enough for us, so here goes.

They got the old mans taller and rubbed it on their faces , arms and neck and legs.

Boy that taller feels good. Don't it Madge? Lesia said

We gona be pretty now, aint we ;Madge said to Lesia? Yeah you look better already, ho Madge?

We gona use that stuff some more times, aint we Madge. Yeah we will, sis. When we take a bath we will rub our selves all over. Come on lets go take us a bath down there in that stream right now.

Lesia and Madge had never used home made soap before, made of hickory ashes lye and parts of hog that was not eaten. Grease from cooking. Every thing was saved that had grease of any kind for that purpose.

Well they had used some now. "Boy, oh boy" were they blistered? Their bodies were red as blood. When they came into view, the old man knew what they had done. He had himself a good laugh

Stole my soap, didn't you ?

Yes we did, said Madge. Ifin we gona stay here and work wens gona take a bath.

Well I wants you to ifin you wants to. Shore will make you smell better. Man youns wusgittin dirty. How long is it been since youns done tooken a bath?

I don't know Madge said as she started into the house.

Git thatar taller bar on thar ar table and rub it good all over youns. Ifin youns dont younsgona be blistered good.

Wens will, said both the girls. As they rubbed down with the taller they realized that theywere using something special. And they would never forget that they were something special to.

Lesia and Madge knew very well that they would be needing some clothes real soon and they did not know where they were coming from, or how they were going to get them If there was a store close by, they were afraid to go in and around where there were people. They knew that they could be recognized and maby put in a home somewhere or some place where they would not be free to do what they wanted to do.

As they sat out side the house, the old man sat with his back against the wall, chewing his tobacco and spitting up a storm. He watched every move the girls made.

As the girls played, Madge threw the ball of straw that she had made then wrapped it tight with long straws and tied it tight so that it would not come apart when it was thrown. The old man reached out and caught it then threw it back to Madge.

Madge walked over near the old man and said mister what is your name?

Mine is Madge and dis heir is Lesia. Yea I done herd youns call eich oder name . Yes I knows whut youns name is. Both aur youins

My name is Lime Carson and I owns this here land wherence never youins staying.

Howence much land does youns own ?

Limb raised his head laughing and said.

Aller this here pretty land over har pointing to the left then pointing to the front of thehouse.then to the right. My Pa and Ma done bough it a long time ago but they died whence I was young and ims done been her ever since. Come over hare the both of youns.

They both hesitated. Come on, come on I aints gona hurt youns I wants to tell younssometin.

The girls looked at each other and went over to where the old man sat. Sot down, sot down. They both sat down and waited for the old man to speak.

I aint got me no body to leave this land to whence never I dies, sos how would youns liketo git it after Ims gone. Whence never air youns going, Mr Limb? Lesia asked.

Well gal Ims gona die some times, Ims an old man. Wens can sees that wit out a doubt. Both the girls agreed. Whens youns gona leave mr limb,? Lesia asked

I aints knowing when Ims gona die. Does youns know whence youns gona die?

Na wens dont knows whens wens gona die. Madge said as she picked the ball up and tried to catch it. Youns wouldnt do notin wit it but sell it and spend the money want youns.

Whut does youns wants usen to do wit it Mr Limb. Dont call me mr Limb, just call me Limb. Dats enough wit us alright. The girls smiled as they looked at each othe.r.

Limb, Madge said hows can usn git some clothes, these clothes wens got own is bout wore out and wens aint got no money and wens aint got no wherence to git none. Ifins wens had some money.

Ise will sees about thatair soon.

The very next morning. Limb got on the old mule , called the girls out and said. Ill be back in a day or two, so you take care of things round here. If something comes up and bothers you sick that dog of yours on them, he will take care of that for you. Theres plenty to eat in there find it eat it all up I dont care I'll git some more, and the old mule started off. As soon as the old man got out of hearing distance, the girls started laughing. They were both laughing at the same thing Wens got it made, aint we Madge? They found something to eat and had lots of fun while Limb was gone.

The water was getting cold in the stream, colder than usual but after all there was a spring above the place where they bathed, a spring furnished water for cooking and drinking and it was always cold.

The girls looked around and found that Limb had been living there for a long time. They believed that he liked to live there and so did they.

Recon where hes gona git some money Lesia? Madge asked. I don't know , recon wensgona git some new clothes, Madge? Asked Lesia.I don't know I hope so Sis she replied. I hope hebmgs us something good to eat. Its been a long time since wens had any thing good to eat, aint it Madge? Im starving to death aint, you Lesia? Plain starved, Madge , just plain starved. Lesia said.Want a piece of pie or some good old candy be good. Uh hu they were both licking their lips.

Madge sat looking at a curtain made of feed sacks that covered a door way. Lesia, Madgesaid, Lesia go to the door and watch for Limb for me Im gona see whats behind that curtain. Ifin you sees him coming. Quietly, altho no one was in miles of there, Madge walked over to the curtain, eased it open and looked in side. She was surprised to see several things covered up, so no dust could get to what ever it was under that cover. She noticed something that made her pullback another curtain made of sacks. There to her surprise was a pedal type sewing machine. Lesia come here> Lesia ran in to see, after she checked once again for Limb. What is it Madge? Lesia, look Madge told her, look at that sewing machine like that air old woman Brown who done lived close to wens, she made her own clothes, Madge went own. Recon wens could make usen some new clothes ifin wens had usn some cloth? Lesia asked with high hopes. Dont know . But betcha I could larn how to do it. I watched old lady brown do it a LOTS. Oh well wens will see in time, Wens will see.

The girls were cooking dried beans and corn bread, it was almost done when Limb come busting in. They though Limb might be thinking he could catch them doing something that he could get on to them for doing. He just stood there in the door way grinning.

Youll come on over here and see whut old Limb done brung youns. Limb pulled out a small paper bag and smiled. Hold out youns hands. As they did ,limb poured out some limmondrops into their hands. One thing that neither of them could stand. They did not like limmondrops, they had tried to eat them before, but they thanked Limb , sat down and ate them any way.

Limb was tickled, it was good to see them eat and enjoy it. "Boy oh boy' the limon drops might have not been good but the girls ate them all up.

After the feast was over. Limb said Gotcha something else to look at too as he opened another large bag.

Two blouses two pairs of britches, some underwear and socks, two pairs of shoes, the works.

I ainta knowing how good they gona fit but them on any way.

The girls were proud of their new clothes. They ran as fast as they could to the branch and took another bath. "Oh no they did not use the lye soap, no sir they just used plain old water.

After they had dried of with the clothes that they had just pulled off, they put the newclothes on, making the remark that they could not have fitted them selves any better if they had gone into town and bough the things to fit there in the store "Oh" they were proud.

When they were back at the house, they both hugged Limbs neck and kissed him and thanked him dearly.

Limb though that was the sweetest thing that had ever happened to him. I aint never had a hug and a kiss before, much obliged to you girls. He said, tickled to the bone.

Yall run now and git them air sacks ofin the mule there is food in them.

The bags were strapped so they would hang on either side of the mule, balanced equally so they would not slide off on either side. The sacks were packed full of good things to eat, after they were cooked. This had been a good day for the children all day long, and they were glad. Now they had lots of good food, new clothes a good place to live and someone to watch over them and love and be loved.

They played and sang as they done their choirs around the house and yard.

As Limb sat with his back resting against the wall of the house, the girls playing with their straw ball they stopped and looked at each other. Probably thinking the same thing or they might have discussed their thoughts, holding hands they slowly walked up to Limb, and said.

Limb, can we call you our Pa? Wens had rather call youns Pa than call youns Limb.

Whetcha wants to do thatair few? Whuts tomatter wit Limb. Nottin they said and walked away.

Limb started laughing to him self, then he said in a kinda loud voice

Show youns can youngons youns already knows that. The both of them turned round.r anback to Limb hugging and kissing him as tho he was their own father.

Madge said to Limb, Pa aint youns reading that air book youns keep looking at?

Sho Limb said whut little I knows how to read.

Will youns show usn how to read. Pa. Wens dont know how to read.

Go there in the house and look under the bed in thatar box and git them books whut Mawus teaching me wit and I will show youns whut Ma learned me.

My Pa and Ma didnt talk like youns does theys says thangs different, from yalls.

Teach us the right way Limb I means Pa.

Dats alright Madge Youns anit been calling me Pa fer long. Youns will leam.

Youns got a box fuller books Pa.

Lesia, Lesia come hare look at whut Pa done got. Books wit pictures , look a here.

Madge hollowed as she went through one or two books

Lesia, Madge said proudly, looks like wens gona leam us somethin, aint wens Lesia?   Ifin Pa will leam mens to read and wright, Ims gona learns all I can.

Is got my self somthin else Im gona shows youns.

Whut is it Pa? Let usn sees it now.

I am, I ams. Limb getting to his feet, come help me wit it madge.

Sho Pa I will helps you. Whut is it?

Youns gona sees, Youns gona sees.

Limb went inside and pulled the curtain open, which Madge had already discovered.Whats this here, Pa.? Talking about the sewing machine, like she had never seen it.

Thatar is a sewing machine, whut people makes clothes wit.

Can I sew on it thatar thang, Pa.? Limb hesitated while Madge hung her head and said something.

Lime continued what he was doing. He brought out, what looked like a heavy woodenbox. Madge looked on.

As he opened the box, whut is thatair thing. Pa.? Limb did not answer, putting a big black wheel on top of another wheel that was inside the box, then turned a crank as to wind up some kind of something that neither of the girls new about, lifted a long arm looking thing and sat it down on the black wheel.

All of a sudden, that box begin to make beautiful music. \

Madge ran out of the door as fast as she could, got Lesia by the hand and was getting out of there.

Lesia acted as she had heard one of them things before.

Limb ran out of the door and said. Wherence never air youns going? It aint notin but a music box. It aint gona hurt youns.

I got some more records come on back in hear and lets play some more music , wensmight dance some to.

Lesia stopped holding on to Madge. Wait Madge , wait I done heard that music afore. Lets go back

No, Madge said, Im scared stiff. I aint never hurd no wooden box make music like that oirbox be doing.

Lets go see, Madge, come own lets go see. That Lesia aint scared of notin.

She shook loose from Madge and ran back in to the house, with Madge right behind her.

Where Madge and Lesia lived there was nothing like that no where around. But Lesia was sure she had heard that sound before.

When they got inside the house Limb had the grafanola playing a beautiful love song, different from the first one that he had played before.

Both of the girls begin to cry, not knowing why perhaps they were still afraid or maby it was the sound of that music that was causing that feeling that one gets with beautiful music.

They sat there for hours just listening to the music, not even as much as moveng. They loved it.

Before long the girls were singing along with the music. They learned every word of every song and memorized them.

Limb, with the book of alphabets, taught the girls how to spell words and put them on paper so they could read them over and over.

Limb was proud of the girls, he could hardly believe it He was raised right here where they were now. Although he never had any teaching except what his mother had taught him. His mother well educated but there was little time left and no one knew. He knew enough to teach the girls enough to get by until there was a school that they could attend with out walking so far to be there. The record player would help them leam the language much better than they were speaking now. Their father had a good education but their mother never had a chance to learn much so the girls learned what their mother had taught them through her daily actions.

When Limb found them, he had heard them talk to each other and he knew their way of talking and the way they used their words. Limb was being as near to their behavior as he could, so as to get closer to them with out going over board, as to say. After a very short while he was beginning to talk like them and what he did not know they were doing the same to him. The girls had discussed the situation before now but neither side had fully understood the meaning of it all as of yet.

Now things were looking up to both sides and every one was enjoying life as a whole.

Every thing was cheap in those days, for instance, two bars of soap for one nickel, a bag of smoking tobacco, ane nickel, a dress for a lady, about one dollar, shoes were about one dollar a pair, or less than two dollars. So what Limbs mother and father left him, he spent very little. Banks were few. I would say there was not a bank within a hundred miles of where Limb lived, soone would have to take care of his or her money.

After Madge learned to sew, she used up all the cloth and thread that Limbs mother had packed back, making hers and Lesia clothes, things were really going well. People would never know that the girls grew up in the sticks where they lived.

There was nothing else to do, so the girls loved and enjoyed what they were doing and where they lived. They did not know what a town looked like, they had never been to town but one day they were to meet the world but at this time they did not care.

Lesia and Madge did not want to leave their home for any reason. Although it was only a log cabin that had been built there for many years, there was their foster father, with plenty of love between the three, that was enough for the both of them.

Where Do We Go From Here

Years seem to fly by. Limb was getting old and the girls were growing up. Every one wondered when their birthday was, but neither knew anything about the other or them selves as far as that goes. Counting back as for as they could Lesia was fifteen and Madge was sixteen. They realized that they were young women now and not just girls. Two beautiful human beings. Their skin was as soft as silk and blemish free. Their hair was black and long, and a fair complexion. Their smiles were growing to be more pleasant than they were when they were rescued. Their manners were like that of a well educated wealthy Lady. As to say Beautiful in every way.

Limb called the girls to his side, as they sat on the porch of the house which they had built out of logs and covered it with moss and sod. A cool place in the summer and a warm place to sit in the winter.

Madge said with her hands together between her knees, whetcha you want Pa?

Limb answered with a grunt and a grin across his face. Go in the house Madge and get that box that's under the bed. Don't you spill what's in it gal, them are my papers that Pa and Ma left me. Madge came out holding it tight with both hands. Whut have you got in that box, Pa.? Im gona show you.

Before I tell you, I want to tell you whut I have been thanking. After we have learned some new things, and words I say lets try to speak better. There's people in town that uses words like we have been using lately.

Lesia Looked at Madge and said. Pa we didn't talk much like this till we come to live with you. Well I know we started talking better for a while but now we done got back to talking that way some more. Well we gona start talking like them town folks right now.

Want to girls?

Sure we do Pa Madge said.

We tried to get you to change the way we were talking long time ago but we din't want to hurt your feelings.

"Yeah' Lesia said so don't talk like we been talking no more. All right? All right they all agreed.

Now you all come up close.

This paper is telling people, that my Pa and Ma give me this land we using now, so it belongs to me.

Now I have got old. So I am giving it to you two girls. Like Pa. Done me.

Both of the girls were laughing as they said almost at the same time. Pa. You did not missa good word, all the time you were talking. You talked different not like we talked.

Well it will take some time to learn all them big words and how to talk like this but we will do it. Want we girls? Patting them on the back as he grinned.

Look here now this is our spending money, I got our other money under the ground. Now Im going to show you where it is so if I die you will have you some spending money. Then you will have money enough to go to school, get you a good education and get you a good job somewhere. Now don't you let some little old boy or any body else take this money from you. Hear me? No body.

"No Pa No sir right Lesia? Ain't no body gona git, "get" Madge broke in. "Get" my money, no sir, Lesia said.

Madge and Lesia knew that to morrow was going to be a big day for them. They had never been to town, never seen inside of a store, "Yes sir" this was going to be a day.

They dressed in what they had the next day, combed their hair after they had scrubed themselves and washed their hair.

Limb was very proud of Lesia and Madge, and he thought they were angles, knowing that they loved him too. They acted like he was his real father, and they were his own two girls. Limb had never been married. He had never had a sweet heart.

Limb, had every thing ready to go when the girls were ready. He put a sack over the mules back and helped the girls on. They had ridden the mule before. That was no problem. Limb led the mule all the way.

As they left the path that ran out of the woods into the road some six miles from where they lived. They talked about the little wild animals that they saw as they came through thewoods.There were several kind of small animals, that they would like to have for pets but I don't think so chep would have probably said since he was jealous of every thing that came between any of the three and him. Limb did not like dogs but he took a liking to chep. There was never any thing said about the girls bringing him along. Both Limb and the girls believed that chep lived with a family who had girls. Chep was a nice dog and had plenty of good dog cense, and he used it too.

As they entered that old dirt road, where perhaps a horseman or wagon had traveled oncein a while, Madge and Lesia knew that they were near something that they wanted to see.

Madge asked Limb, Pa she said, how far is it now?

Brush your clothes off they are covered with dust, the both of you and comb your hair. I am going to get you a mirror so you can see what you look like, and watch your selves grow prettier all the time. Madge and Lesia liked that. They had not seen them selves except in the water at the wash hole in a long time. They wondered if they had changed all that much since they had seen themselves in a mirror.

What's a mirror? Lesia asked Madge.

It a piece of glass that you can see your self in, Lesia. as she turned slightly to look at her.

We haven't seen any thing, have we Madge, not much, Madge agreed. Actually they did not remember any thing much that they had seen. Now every thing was changing so much in the last few months.

Limb smiled as he said .Look girls, there she is., there's town. That big house is the courthouse where we are going. Pa, Lesia said, as she shrunk down real low, I am scared I am not going up there. I want to go home. Come on Madge, let's get out of here I don't like towns.

Here girls, here's you some money you can buy something with.

Here's you a dollar a piece, you can buy a lots with that. So buy any thing you want to that cost a dollar.

Pa. They said together, we don't know what we want, what are we going to but?

I'll show you and I will be with you when you go into a store. You might want a nickles worth of candy for all I know.

Madge said, I had some candy one day but I don't know what it looked like now.

I'll show you what to buy if you don't know what you want.

As they approached the front of the store where Limb traded, he helped the girls off of the mule, and they strolled in. Git that hound dog outa here, the store manager screamed out. Yes sir Madge said as she turned to chep and told him to go out side to wait. Chep turned slowly around and started out of the door where he lay down in front of the door.

That dog minds you like he was your own child. How did you ever get him to do that.

A smart dog, chep is, Madge said.

Sure is the manager replied.

What can I do for you, asked the manager?

Come here P Madge called to Limb.

What's this Pa?

That's candy, Madge. You want some of that?

Chocolate drops, they are good too.

Limb told the manager to let them have a dimes worth of candy each, so he did.

Limb got another dimes worth for him self.

They all went on the out side, sat on the edge of the porch and enjoyed the whole thing..

After the candy feast, the girls had candy all over their hand and face. Should have seen chep licking chocolate I don't believe he had candy before.

As they stopped at the watering trough to wash their hands. Limb told them to come along to the court house.

The clerk of court and the judge helped to make out the deed to the girls. Limb gave everything he owned to the them. Of course they did not know what to do with it just now, so the Judge said just let it be until later knowing that Limb would handle things.

When they arrived home from their day in town, every one was tired. There was groceries, some of which the girls had never seen, they did not know whether to eat such stuff or to let chep have it but they learned something new every day.

There was more to do and leam about in this place than in place one could think of.

After supper, sitting waiting for the sun to disappear from a lovely blue sky, talking about every thing that happened in town that day. What they had seen and what was given to them. They couldn't love Limb enough to pay for the good times they had.

Come morning. Limb said with a grin all over his face, old Limb is gonna show you girl show to get rich quick if you want to. Both of the girls crawled up in his lap, begging him to tell them what it was.

Not till morning, not till morning, all day is what it takes. All day. The night was long , no one could sleep. Lets do it now Pa. The girls begged Limb.

Not till morning, go to sleep you will need all the rest you can get when you start working tomorrow. Go to sleep , its getting late you know.

Every one went to sleep and the morning came before they knew it. The sun had long came up and not a cloud in the sky.

Every one hurried up, had a good breakfast and stood waiting for orders to do what everi t was they were going to do to get rich In their hearts and mind they knew that they were already rich. Limb saw to that yesterday but that was not what they wanted to right now but to do whatever it was to do together. Madge had boiled some coffee And made some biscuits then buttered them with butter she had just churned. Limb told the girls to take what was left, wrap it up in the sacks that they brought things home from town in and bring it along with them.

At that moment they knew that there was an all day something in store for them. As they went out of the door. Limb turned around and reached over head for some large shiny pans, that was laying just under the top and above the sealing of the house.

"Pa what is that"The girls were puzzled. Were they going to cook, take it into town and try to sell it? We don't know we will just wait and see.

No body talked much, no one knew what to talk about, just wait on Limb.

Limb locked the door and they started out through the woods.

"All right Pa.? We are ready. Tell us now what we are going to do to get rich.

WE are almost there girls. We are almost there. See that row of green over there? YeahThere. Yeah that's a stream Pa. We crossed it coming to your house. Remember? Right, you remember well. That was a long time ago. Girls, this is your land. You know? You got a lot of it.

Lets get down by the stream. There, we will start right there where that sand is. "Now" I'm going to show you how to do it, so listen well and it will be no trouble. See? Watch me now.

Limb got his pan full of sand and water. He began to swerve it around and around. Letting a little of the water slip over the edge of the pan, with out letting to much of the sand get out.

After several swerves he let some more sand slide out. He done this until all the sand was gone.

After all the sand was gone. Limb, held the pan with one hand, took the other hand with the fore finger just inside the pan, raked some thing that looked like mud out of the pan, and said. Look here girls, there's plenty of dust here so get busy

Limb pulled something out of the bag that he was carrying, it was a small bag made from rabbit hide and raked the mud looking stuff into it.

Here, he said, is some bags for you to put your gold dust in. Put them in your pocket you might need more than one in days to come.

Pa what is that stuff, Madge asked. I know you told us gold dust but what is gold dust?

"Man" you girls are dumb. You don't know what gold is?

No, Pa we don't know nothing but what you have taught us. Remember.

Well you know it is better than money and you shore know what money is, don't you? Pa. You mean we can buy candy and things with this mud that you are putting in that bag?

Sure can its just like money, that's what you have been eating off of. That candy, you bought it with some gold dust that Pa. And Ma. Had changed into money a long time ago.

Pa. I don't have me any yet, Madge said kinder un decided whether she liked this idea or not.

Look, Limb said as he stuck his hand over into Madge's pan, pulling out a pebble looking rock. Man look at that as big a nugget as I ever seen. He examined it well and gave it to Madge. Well am I doing good or what. Look at the mud I got in my pan. That is gold dust Madge, yeah you are doing good.

What about you Lesia? What have you got? Look Madge, she has lots of gold too.

"Boy" we are doing good, you all keep up the good work and we will be going into town soon to change our gold dust in for money.

Those words really set the girls on fire, they begin to work harder than before. Getting rich was their desire, thinking perhaps that some day there might be enough for Ma. And Pa but no, that could never happen it would only make things worse for Pa. And ma would get Pa to bring her more liquor and that would not be any better for them, to bring her more. "Oh shucks, get that off your mind, Madge and pan for gold for your selves. Pa could learn to take care of himself. You did it, and so could Pa.

So this is gold dust Pa. So what Lesia asked as she sat on a rock ringing wet. I haven't understood what this is all about.

Lesia, You take that stuff that you just put into your bag, take it to a place where they buy gold dust and get money for it.

Well, how much do Im get for what I got now?

The sun was setting, the girls were tired and ready to go home. The trip home was not all that far but it seemed much father than it was. The supper was good and each of them were starved. It had been a long time since either of them worked. 0 h, but they would be getting use to work-ing when they found out that there was good money in what they were doing.

After supper, Limb called the girls over to the table where he had sat the box that contained their spending money.

Sit down. Limb told them. I want you to know just what you are looking for.

Do you see this piece of paper, like I gave you at the store to buy candy with? Uh hu, they answered. Just like I told you before, this is a one dollar bill. Yes sir we remember what that is. Well, see this, this is a dime. It takes ten of these to make one of these dollar bills. Now this is a nickel, it takes two of these nickels to make one of these dimes. And twenty of these nickels to make one of these one dollar bills. Now it will take ten of these one dollar bills to make one of these ten dollar bills. Do you know what I am saying? We think so, the girls nodded as they spoke.

Here you both take one each of these pieces of money and leam all about it. Do it now you are going to need what you leam, real soon.

While the girls were looking the money over. Limb was bringing out of the box several bags, containing gold dust, and nuggets. Limbs Father and Mother had been panning for gold many years. They did not spend no more money than they had to so Limb would have money when he was old, and could not work. They raised enough on the farm to live very well and have money to put away for spending money. That was what

Limb was calling their spending money.

As the girls watched Limb drag out more of the money out of the box, they noticed some large coins that they did not recognize. What are these. Pa? The girls asked.

This is a quarter, takes four of these to make one dollar. These are half dollars, takes two of them to make one dollar, and this big one is a one dollar piece. You can spend them like you would a dollar bill. I was going to wait till you had learned the others coins first but now just take these too and leam all you can about money.

The morning came fast and every one was ready to go to work. Now Limb grunted as he rose to his feet. Lets go to work, right now girls, right now.

The girls scampered out of the house, pounding on their pans and singing all the way to the stream.

Pa and Ma, made all their spending money panning for gold, we can to. Limb was trying to keep the girls in a good working mood, that they might want to carry own. He showed them how to fill their pans the best way he knew so it would be easy to handle. It is really tiresome to lift that pan full of sand all day long, but so far there was no complaint.

Madge done just what Limb told her to do, swerve the pan, round and round. Had already done this yesterday and it worked so there was no trouble in doing it now. Letting the water swerve over the top of the pan to let the water roll out the edge of the pan instead of letting it slosh out and losing the gold dust that lingered in the pan. It would go to the bottom or settle in the little groves in the side of the pan like it suppose to do. Any way you could get it was good

They panned for a long time and did not get any thing so they moved on down the stream. Suddenly as they were all shaking their pans. Limb hollowed out to Madge, who was a short Distance up stream. Wait a minute look here Madge, here's a nugget as large as a quarter> That's the biggest nugget I have ever seen.

That's gold?

Just like the one you found yesterday, only bigger.

Lesia, have you got any thing yet?

Naw, Lesia replied kinda disappointed.

You'll get something before long now. Limb told her. There's plenty of gold here, You just have to find it.

Look Pa, look. Another gold nugget like the other one, ain't it Pa?

Shore is. Limb assured her.

See, I told you, there's plenty of gold here.

How much is this one gonna be worth , Pa?

Limb checked it over good and said. Looks like its gonna be about two ounces Madge. Go own, get all you can.

Lisia threw all the sand out of her pan and gave op. I give up, I'm quitting.

No, Lesia, no don't quit now. You'll fing something soon.

Limb looked at Lesia's pan. Look here girl, look at all that dust around the edge of your pan, hand it to me.

Limb took the pan and with his finger raked the dust from around the edge of the pan.

You have done better than me. We'll all be rich, here give me that bag. How did you know the gold was here, Pa? How did you leam where to look for it?

Well this is why Ma and Pa settled here because they found this stream with gold in it.They though that there was a gold vein near here but they never found anything, if there was ever any thing.

There is more gold here than I ever though there might be..

We will all get what we can this the best job you can find around here. That Lesia was quiet, she was getting that gold dust.

If any body ask you where you got this gold dust, you can tell then that you got it upstream of the river, about six miles from here., but nobody will ever ask you where you got the it.

Wens done got about six ounces of gold dust this morning. Limb told the girls.

Pa. You told us to stop saying words like ,wens and youns. Remember?

Shore do we got to be careful, and we go to study some more to night. So we had better go home now.

Lesia, You got a lot of dust, didn't you. Uh ho, I did almost as good as you did Madge.

We will do better tomorrow. We will have to get all we can while we are getting good runs. one.

They all cleaned their pans and went back home. The day had been a long one but a good one.

That's all the girls could talk about while they fixed supper, and Limb milked the cow.

The night was closing in fast, so Limb lit the lamp. Every one gathered

Around the little table with their books and studied as hard as they could.

Chep lay in the door way watching for a squirrel or a rat coon to come by so he couldchase them.

The only school house around was ten or fifteen miles a way. If one got an education, they got it at home. So were trying to leam what ever they could.

The graffa phone was a big help. Although the songs were very old but that was all they had. There were lots of records, so they played the ones they liked, singing along with the musicl earning every word by hart and remembering them well.

Time passed, every day they gathered more dust and nuggets.

Going to town was getting more frequent, almost every week they went in.

Limb bough more clothes and cloth for Madge to make their clothes from patterns which Limb had bough. Some times it was hard to figure out haw to make a garment from a pattern but she always got it right.

Every thing the girls did they tried to do it as near what they though was right as possible. Im sure that they was determine to some day see their parents again and their desire were to make them as proud as possible of what they had achieved. Some times they would wake up at night crying about the loss of their parents and would give their lives to hold them just for a few seconds. Although they though it would never happen for fearing that the girls would never be found.

The girls were beginning to be watched by young men and they were looking more closely at the young men. Some times they would stop and talk for a few minutes, then on with their business.

Reaping The Harvest

Days passed the girls seemed not to understand the boys at all. They had began to read more about people and leam more about how they lived, and what life was all about. They had never been to school but they had learned much more than some children who had had much teaching. Never been in the presence of people enough to leam how to enjoy their company. Their in life seemed to be how to leam to leam and they learned every thing that they could their way.

Grading each others papers then asking each other questions and drilling till everything was learned by hart.

Any thing any one wanted to know about the Bible and what was in it, just ask one of the girls they could answer the question.

Their little house to some people, would be just a shack but no, it was their home and they were proud of it. What other people might have though, was another subject, because other people had never seen their place. If questions were asked, no one had an answer. So time went on and the girls were happy.

For a long time nearly every day they would go out and pan for gold. Already they had several sacks apiece but they seemed to never get enough.

One day Limb told the girls to get their gold dust to gather. Then he showed them how to make a strap so they could carry all their gold without straining them selves. While they went to a town a ;long way off. To exchange it for money. The bank in that town bough gold dust at a good price. The girls were amazed when they learned that a sack of gold dust was worth a fortune. With in its self. When they learned that one ounce of gold, was less than one tea spoon full. They realized the several bags of gold dust was worth lots of money then there was the bags that Limb had thrown in with there's.

Limb put his hand down into his bag and pulled out two small guns, looked at the girls and said. Today, is what I taught you how to shoot a gun for. You will need some protection when we start home. We could be held up and robbed. I hope nothing like this happens, but it could and now you will have a chance to get away.

Putting the guns away in their own bags, as they walked along noticing that they were not so heavy as to be noticed. Stopping now and then on the side of the road, that was made only with hands, picks and shovels for wagons pulled by horses and mules. The wealthy people from around the country side used their buggies for traveling, or road their horses. You could see most of all their way of traveling by foot or a plain old worn out mule. Any was good if you had to walk home with animal feed or a months supplies of groceries. Most of the people who farmed did not worry about raising to much grain or vegetables that had to be transported to other parts of the country, because there was no way to keep it from spoiling on its way to market, so whatever they needed could be found in town.

Madge and Lesia always rode the mule while Limb led him own. The bags that held their clothes, or any thing they had to carry, hang off both sides of the mule, so they did not have to tote them.

In town, the mule would eat better than he would eat at home. In a stable with other animals, there were plenty of straw and corn for the animals to munch on,

After the three of them took care of their business, they spent the night in a little wooded area on the out skirts of town. No one bothered them, they were quiet and did not move around to much.

It was a long way home but no one bothered them in any way. As they traveled they talked about how they could take care of their money and build a better place to live, where they could be with people and stop living in the woods like hermits. If we spend some of our money we could always get more gold dust. They came to a conclusion of what they were going to do. Build a small house for the three of them, then build a road into town from the new house.

Resting for a while when they reached home, done the choirs, milked the cow and went to bed early. Come morning every one was up ready to go into town. Finding a one horse wagon, loading it with lumber, some brick, some sacks of cement, nails, tin for the top, any thing they could thank of for the job and hurried home. They couldn't wait to get started on their new home. Picking out a good spot was not so hard. The new tools that was bough came in handy since Limb's tools were old and dull.

A few days passed, the brick for the foundation was finished. Limb went into town for supplies while the girls worked on the house doing the things that Limb had showed them to do.

Finally after about six months the house was, the house was ready to move into. It could be finished while they enjoyed being so close to their new place.

There was a room for each of them. A kitchen, one sitting room and two large porches. There was a small room on the end of one of the porches ton be used for a bath room. There was no toilet or shower, not even running water but there was a well dug just off the porch with a hand pump, so there was plenty of fresh water. No more going to a spring waiting for the water to clear up so it could be drank. The toilet was out some twenty feet from the house that would be enjoyed because the one at Limbs old place was a mess. A huge chimney in the middle of the house with a fireplace in every room. Wood was plenty fill so they would be warn in winter time.

New furniture beds, chest, dressers especially in the girls rooms, with huge mirrors so the girls could fix them selves up real pretty any time they felt like doing so.

There was a large flat iron stove put in the kitchen that would be very much appreciated. Madge and Lesia, remembered their ma and pa had two beds in their home, the mattress was some feed sacks sewed to gather and stuffed with fresh wheat straw. "Oh" but nothing like this. Their mattress was pretty and filled with soft cotton. Every thing was planed to each ones notion. No one had any thing to gripe about, because it was their own doings that made it better. So every thing was well.

All the people around town noticed their appearance and wondered where their money was coming from. So they continued raising chickens and selling eggs. Some times Limb would take milk into town and sell it and buy it up in groceries. There was vegetable in the spring to sell. Rabbits, squirrels, possum, coon, that furnished fur and hides. No one ever expected that there was gold on the place. So there was no reason why they should spend the money that they were trying to save, or spend their gold dust and run the risk of giving their secret away. They just left every thing at the cabin until they were ready to bring it home to the new house.

Madge used her bedroom in the summer time for a sewing room where she made her and Lesia's clothes, from patterns which she had bought at the dry goods store in town. She also found some pull op and down to go on the windows in the house. After she had made and finished the curtains and hung them on every window, that little house was beginning to look like a rich mans little house. It really was but they did not realize it. They had gobs of land, anew home, a stream full of gold, and a nice little farm to furnish plenty of fresh vegetables and anything that would grow that they might eat. No one knew just how it kept on going, but no one seemed to care.

Each time they were in town what ever was bough Limb was always called to pay the bill. Limb would take out a little black snap to gather pocket pouch slowly open it finger around with the change, like he was trying to come up with enough money to pay for the bill. Some times he would have to put the item back until I can sell some more eggs, but right now this is all I got. So they would put the item back until they had the money. Some times he would buy a nickels worth of kerosene for the lamps. Sound stupid? But that is how Ma and Pa taught him. They did not want the people to get the wrong impression of their buying power. Limbs M and Pa tried to save for another day, even if they did have plenty. His Mother always had new clothes, because like Madge she knew how to sew and make her own clothes and his Pa's shirts and under ware.

People in town would get Madge to make their clothes. Wedding gowns and things that they could not make them selves. She made enough money alone to satisfy the peoples suspicious ideas.

No one ever tried to find out where the girls came from or any thing about them, but Limb was growing old now and he knew that they had to have some one to take care of them after he had grown to old to do the choirs like milk the cow, which was a necessity for country folk. Or to cut wood for the winter and there was wood to be used for cooking. So he begin to fix his self up with good clothes and what ever with out touching their savings or their spending money back at the old home, which they kept up like some one lived there. It wasn't to far away so it was no

Limb would go into town, sit around looking for some one to introduce the girls too. Actually he was looking for some young man that

Madge would marry and make them both a good home. That was his most worries, trying to provide for the girls future after he was gone, and he seemed to cherish that more than any thing he did.

One evening as he sat in a bar, next door to the dry good store where Madge bough her sewing supplies, the owner of the store came in and sat down on the stool next to Limb. He looked Limb over good and said to him. You are the father of the two young women that buy a lot of cloth and sewing supplied at my store. Right? Yes I am. Why, Limb asked rapidly? Well I though you were. We are having a party Saturday night, why don't you and tour daughters come. We would be honored to have all of you. "Well" we might just do that. What time does your party start. Sir? Oh I think we will start with the music, around seven o'clock. Will you three come? Just might, just might, and continued drinking his coffee.

When the store owner left the bar, limb hurried out to break the news to Madge and Lesia. They did not knows what to say or do. They had never been to a party before just heard about them and what they did.

Trying to dance to the music on their recorder was hard to do, but they got themselves anew kind of swing of their own. Dancing to slow and fast music was fun even if they did not know how to do it. But they were ready come Saturday night.

Madge made then both new party dresses, they were lovely and ready to go two or three days early.

Limb got dressed up and come in for the girls to comment on whether he was properly dressed or not, and if he would fit in with the town people. They made sure of that.

Everything was happening so fast and they were ready, but they did not know if the boy sand girls danced to gather or not, but if they did then they would leam.

Saturday morning came. When the girls got out of bed , Limb had left for town to go to the stables to rent a two seat buggy and a high stepping horse to pull it with. When he came in home with that rig the girls were thrilled cause that was new to them. They came out running to see that thing and look it over.

Pa, Lesia said. Can we sit in it for a while? Of course you can, come on lets take a ride, do you want to? Yes they both hollered out in a loud voice. Shedding a few tears of happiness, Wondering if it was plain luck or was it meant to be

They were thinking of their real Pa and Ma. What if they could see us now sitting here in this huge buggy pulled by a beautiful high stepping horse.

They wasn't down grading their parents, although they had been treated awful in their younger days but that was over. Perhaps never to see them again. Makes no difference They both loved then both. They were proud that it happened this way for pa's sake Knowing that he loved their mother. As the tears ran off their face they couldn't help smiling as they walked to the house with their arms around Limb. Talking to each other later on that day, Madge told Lesia, Lets forget every thing for the moment and lets except it as it is. If we don't, we might loose everything and well never have another chance. Do you remember the bible, we learned from Limb that there is some one who loves all of us and will take care of us as long as we believe and we do believe. Don't we Lesia? We know we couldn't have done this alone. Madge, do you believe believe that Limb is the man that the Bible tells about. We couldn't have done it without him. Could we Madge? No Lesia We were on our last stand, we had done all we could do then along came Limb, but that is not the Man the bible speaks of. That Man is Jesus, so Limb says and Limb knows cause he reads that book all the time. Do you remember how he makes us bow our heads down when he talks to that man that he reads about. Yeah, Do you think he might meet him someplace when we are not around, Madge? Lesia asked. I don't know Lesia but lets get him to talk about him some more when were resting and read out of that book to. I like that book Dont You?

Yeah I like that book.

Pa and Ma couldn't have fed us you know Lesia ? As we have discussed it before there was no work for Pa to do to get money for groceries so I guess we would have been dead now if Limb had not come along. Instead of them talking care of us, We are talking care of them. It might not seem that way but they don't have to worry about us. After all these years if we couldn't have made it, we would have not been around.

Lets don't mention it again because they think we are dead. If they had have wanted to find us they could have. I'm afraid if they found out about us now there would trouble and they would get everything we have. We would be back right where we started from, Mama would drank every thing we have up in whiskey. Lesia we don't know any body but Pa. Limb, our pa for longer than we knew our real Pa. For get every thing about the past and gather the faturae anyway we can get it.

Well. we were just feeling sorry for them so I want mention it again. I promise

The girls hurried Limb up to eat breakfast with them since it was getting late in the morning. They discussed several things at the table making plans for their part at the party

Every thing was sat and ready for them to go. When they figured out about the right time that they should arrive at the party. Being prompt was their desire and after they had pushed theirs elves every minute to do what was prompt was all they wanted.

he horse stopped at the door where the party was already in progress. Limb helped the girls out of the buggy and escorted them to the door-steps held their arms as they walked up the steps to the porch.

Was this magic or were they dreaming asking each other as they walked up the steps. Looking like queens in their pretty new party dresses. They had no jewelry at all. No one had ever mentioned jewelry to either of them. Diamonds and pearls were unknown of so they did not mention jewelry. They had seen pictures of jewels, they just were not interested at all.

In the house they were met by several of the towns people who had seen them several times in town. Being escorted to a seat near the wall in the ball room, much different from their new home but not as lovely, they though.

The band started playing, boys and of all ages began dancing, no one asked the girls to dance. Madge went over to Lesia, and said.

Miss Lesia, May 11 have this dance?

Tickled to her shoes, giggled and said.

Why of course My dear, come lets dance.

As they begin to dance, just trying was fun. They only knew what Limb had taught them.Limb learned from his Mother and Father, long years ago. As the girls danced around in the old home ,on a dirt floor and listened to the record player. The music now was much different than it was back then, but they were having a good time. Limb sat there by the wall taking it all in.

Yes he remembered back then when he was a small child, how it was with his Mother and Father That's all he knew, was what he learned from them. Nothing like this had ever happened to him before.

All the pretty things that was in the house where they were. In fact he had never been in a house like this before. Just a small log cabin or two, where some of their friends lived, years ago. Limb could not believe he was here- All that good wine he had never tasted before going to his head. "Aw" but that was alright the girls were having fun. That was his only ambition, to maket he girls happy. They had given him more plea-sure than they would ever know. Just having them around was the whole world to him. Limb would never know his influence on two beautiful, precious members of Gods family.

Very shortly the young boys caught on. They begin to each other, while looking at Madge and Lesia. Seriously. While the dancers rested for another set, two young men approached them. Being more surprised than proud, as the young men asked for the next dance. Of course we will dance with you, want we Lesia" Sure we will. The music began they got to their feet and began dancing across the floor. The young men were very good dancers, that seemed to be what the girls wanted. Learning how to follow their leader, wasn't so hard and they were beautiful to watch.

The time was growing late, the ban was playing their goodnight song. Madge's friend asked if he could see her again. I don't know I'll let you know as soon as I ask my Daddy. So it went as that.

Lesia did not want to see her boy friend again, she did not like boys at that time. Each time she was ask if they could come see her.

Lance Seemore, was the boys name that danced with Madge at the party., learned that she came int the store for her supplies, managed to see her every time she came into the store. Lance asked if he could see her at her home. She told him that he could. After the first visit, they came frequently.

One Sunday evening. Lance came to see Madge in his buggy pulled by a beautiful white horse and asked if Madge could go for a ride. Limb told him to ask Madge if she cared to go. If she wants to go then she has my permission. So they drove away.

The sun was setting in a flame of glow when Lance and Madge re-turned. Lesia and Limb was setting by the window waiting for their return.

Here they come, Lesia, said Limb, Here they come.

Madge looked so happy as they drove up. Lance climbed out of the buggy, and helped Madge to the ground. As they stood there, looking at each other. Limb pulled Madge up close to his cheek, held her tight and softly kissed her then let her go.

Madge turned from Lance and started up the path toward the house smiling and humming like she had never done before.

Poor Lesia turned loose the curtain, tears pouring down her face, grabbed Limb around the neck and said,

Madge is in love, ain't she Pa ain't she? I'm afraid she is said Lesia, said Limb. "Oh "Pa. This is the beginning ain;t it Pa?

Beginning of what Lesia'

The beginning of the, sob, sob. Beginning of, The End

Annie The Good Witch

Our first encounter with Annie, happened when I was a young boy. We thought she was gone from our lives forever. We found out that she stayed close by and some times today when I see a big black dog I think of Annie, The Good Witch.

ANNIE THE GOOD WITCH

As I sometimes pass the old house where I was born, I'm astonished to see it is still standing. It even looks the same as it has for many years. I enjoy so much to still look into the window that faces the road and think back to the years to when I was a small child. I can still remember some of the people that I waved to as they passed up and down the road. This was one of my favorite things to do. Every day I spent many hours doing just that.

I remember one morning, the clouds were low, heavy and blustery, the wind was blowing like one would not believe. The winter months had just begun, the crops had all been taken care of. Every body was glad to see the cooler weather come. Of course the work had not ceased as of yet but it was getting there. No one was working today because everyone was expecting bad weather with lots of wind and rain.

Mama was in the kitchen doing the dishes while the rest of the family was in the sitting room where the front window was. Dad was standing by the window watching the weather. Suddenly Dad called Mama to the window. He was peering out like he was amazed at what he saw. We all rushed to the window to see the excitement that they were looking at. There coming down the road was a wagon with a woman and man sitting on the seat. The man was very different looking and just unpleasant to look at. His clothing was in rags, his coat was torn, his beard was long and his hair streamed down his back. The woman had long stringy hair with clothing as raggedy as the man's. They were a sign to see, driving an old skinny mule that looked as if he had not eaten in days. The wagon was a wreck with the sides all hanging down, the wheels rolling crooked and wobbled as they turned. About ten feet behind was the poorest dog I have ever seen. What was once a fine dog for hunting was now just a worn out red bone hound which looked starved half to death. The old mule was walking so slowly he would make one tired just to watch.

As the wagon passed by the house Old Blue and the other dogs lying in the yard did not even bark as the wagon passed. This was very unusual as no one knew why the dogs did not even bark. Dad asked Mama if she knew why our dogs had not attacked that skinny dog. Mama answered that she had no idea in amazement. She said she had never seen anything like it before. Dad started to say do you suppose, but then as he looked around at the children he cut the question short. He said maybe it was just someone who was lost. We watched the wagon continue down the road until they were lost around the curve.

Hunting Season Was At Hand

We spent most of the day talking about the hunting season, checking out the dogs and the hunting gear. Of course the strangers were a big part of our thoughts. People in those days were very frightened of people that they did not know. Indians and gypsies were always camping up and down the road trying to sell anything that they might get hold of, like apples, oranges, nuts and other items that people needed but could not get at the local grocery store. They would trade anything for chickens, flour, meal or pork after the hog killing weather began. Although every one knew about these people, they still kept a watch on their livestock and whatever they had that could be stolen at night.

There were witches in those days and everyone was afraid of them. They would stay close by wherever they called home and we certainly stayed far away from them. You could find the witch sitting near the hut or where they were staying, cooking their food, mostly boiling soup or porridge. The warlock, that was the witch's husband, I guess he never worked but just sat around with the witch. We always left the witches alone or anyone we thought was a witch. There were two kinds of witches, good and bad. People would swear they would see the bad witches flying through the air on their brooms. The wore long black dresses which flapped in the wind, with tall black hats on their heads and high topped shoes that went halfway up their legs. They were certainly scary to see.

The good witch was quite different. They were beautiful to look at as their faces were smooth and most had wavy black hair. Their lovely eyes would follow you everywhere you went. Women were jealous of them because they were so beautiful and were afraid that the witches might steal their husbands. The witches never had a chance in life as there was no one that would give them a job so they just had to do the best they could. Their suspected power was all they had. They seemed to get along just fine. Life in those days for the people who were afraid was verymiserable.

A few days passed and everything seemed fine. The strange people who had passed the house had been forgotten. One night Dad called Mama to the window in their bedroom. All the children knew there must be something special to see so we all ran to the window. "Mama," Dad asked, "when have you seen a light in that old shack down there?" Mama slowly shook her head with a worried look upon her face. "I don't know, but it's been a long, long spell. Get all the children into the house, quickly." Dad answered, "Yes Mama, they are all in here now." Mama, sitting on the side of the bed, looked up and said, "You children must be very careful not to go near that old shack down there. Now there ain't nothing to be afraid of, but you never can tell. Here me now?" "Yes Mama," we all agreed and went off to bed.

One evening Mama cooked a rice pudding and roasted a large pan of peanuts. We were waiting for the peanuts to get done when a loud knock at the door startled everyone. Dad looked around and told all the kids to go into the bedroom while he answered the door. Lo and behold there was the woman and man who had ridden by in the wagon. Dad was startled but he said, "come in, come right in. Mama, we got company." Mama came to door wiping her hands on her apron. "Howdy," she said, "come on in and have a seat." Dad introduced himself and stuck out his hand. The man stuck out his hand and said, "My name is Rufus and this is Annie. We are staying down in the old house for a spell." "Pleased to know you all," both Mama and Dad greeted them with pleasure. Dad called for all of us children to come and introduce ourselves to Rufus and Annie. We did but we were scared half to death. We listened while Dad and Rufus talked. Annie and Rufus kept looking toward the kitchen door, almost going out of their minds. Mama noticed right off and called Dad to the kitchen. "Dad," she said, "did you notice the look on their faces as they smelled the rice pudding?" Dad said, "Sure did Mama, sure did. What are we gonna do? Mama said, "Ask them to eat some and we will eat the parched peanuts later. Is that all right with you?" Dad said, "Sure, I'll call them into the kitchen." Mama said, "Oh, Dad, take the peanuts out to the young ones and let them eat the peanuts while we entertain the company." Dad said, "Rufus, Annie, you all come into the kitchen for some pudding." No sooner was that said than they were in the kitchen. "Have a seat folks and let's have the blessing," said Dad. When Dad had given thanks for the food. Mama served the pudding. Boy did they dig right in! Rufus ate until he was well filled and probably could still have eaten more. Of course the children did not get any pudding so Mama said she would bake another. We were all having a good time. I have never had company to enjoy themselves as much as Annie and Rufus did. They really felt at home. I do not believe that they had never eaten any parched peanuts before. They did that night and I do believe they enjoyed themselves.

Here's Where The Fun Really Started

Dad was a musician. He could play the fiddle and several other instruments. On Saturday nights he was always invited out to someone's house to play for a dance or a sing along, just anything to have a good time. Someone would said, "Dad, play the fiddle and let's sing some country songs." So Dad would get out the fiddle and begin to play. We sand and the whole bunch danced. Although Annie and Rufus did not know how to square dance they learned fast. After they got tired of dancing and singing, we all sat around and talked. Dad invited them to a dance that we were having. Annie shyly said, "We don't have anything to wear to a party." "Well," Mama said, "We'll just have to do something about that. Won't we. Dad?" "Why yes, Mama, what will that be?" Dad asked. Mama got to her feet and went into the bedroom where her things were. Soon she called Annie to come into the bedroom. Both Mama and Annie came out modeling the clothes that Mama had found. Some of the clothes she had worn before the children were born. Now the clothes were too small for her but they fit Annie. Pa found a pair of homespun pants and Grannie had made for him that fit Rufus perfectly. Now everything was set for the dance. None of us could define just what made the evening so enjoyable but we knew there must be something there that we couldn't understand.

The evening was gone, it was after ten o'clock and the company had just left. Strange but I don't think they ever told us their last names. All we had heard was Annie and Rufus. Suddenly Old Blue let out a bark we had heard many times before. He had smelled a possum. "Let's go get that possum, boys," Dad called. The dogs ran all night but never treed the possum. Now things were beginning to look a little strange. Earlier when the company was there with their dog none of our dogs had anything to do with their dog. When Mama threw the scraps out our dogs just let their dog eat it all with no growls or barking.

At the end of the week, late Friday night. Old Blue took another notion to go hunting. Off we go into the woods. Old Blue was on his toes that night. He treed possum after possum. Suddenly all the dogs gathered around and lay down as if they needed to rest. We all gathered together and stared. Everyone spoke in real low voices so no one could hear us. But we all knew there was no one around. Thomas, my oldest brother, whirled around as if he had heard the devil. The dogs never whined. "What was going on?" one of the brothers wondered. We were all shaking and scared to death. Shucks we knew there was no such things as ghosts even though people were afraid of them anyway. We knew that there were witches and that they had been caught doing things that seemed impossible and put in prison. Thomas got to his feet and went to the edge of the woods. He held his lantern high and Rufus appeared out of no where, smiling. He said he had been there for a short while. He said, "Howdy boys ,it sounded like Old Blue had a possum up a tree. My old dog has been feeling poorly lately and we haven't had a possum this year. Could you spare one?" Thomas looked around at the rest of us but no one said a word. I knew what he had in mind when he handed the sack with the possums in it. He knew if Rufus stuck his hand in that bag he would get bitten by that big old possum inside. Rufus took the bag and opened it so he could get his hand inside. He felt in the sack for several seconds smiling as felt the possums. Rufus certainly knew what he was doing as he brought out the biggest possum we had caught. That possum wasn't blowing or even moving. Possums just don't do that and when you are bitten by a possum you know you have been bitten. It hurts awful for a long time. The teeth go so deep you bleed as bad as if you'd cut your finger off. Rufus raised the possum up to the light, grinned, and asked, "can I have this one?" "Yes, you can have it, Rufus, is one enough?" we cried. He smiled again and said, "One is enough" as he walked back into the woods. We did not see him again that night. We did not even want to see him any more that night. We went home fast. After we told Dad what had happened, he was more suspicious than ever.

The Saturday Night Dance Coming Up

Everybody was ready to go to the dance about sundown. We knew it was pretty far from the house so we dressed for the cool night. We hitched up our best two mules to the wagons, filled the lanterns with oil, put pine knots into the pot to burn incase the weather turned cold. We reached the old house where Annie and Rufus lived. Rufus was ready to go but Annie was not going. No one questioned Rufus as to why Annie was not going and he did not mention it anymore. I don't remember Rufus ever speaking after he said howdy to us. Off to the dance we went.

Everybody was there waiting for the fiddler to show up. They were ready to go so Dad began to play. Rufus pulled up a chair by the fireplace where he could watch the dancers and punch at the fire. He got a drink of punch, crossed his legs and settled down for the night. Everyone was having fun and not watching what other folks were doing. I crawled up by other side of the fireplace near Rufus. As we sat there a huge dog came up the steps as there was no porch on the house, laid down in front of Rufus and put his head on his feet. Rufus looked down at the dog and kicked it. The dog just crawled back and laid its head again on Rufus' foot. Rufus reached over the side of the fireplace and picked up the fire iron. He stood up and hit the dog across the back as hard as he could. The dog tried to crawl off but it was hurt too bad. Rufus kicked it as hard as he could in the side and the dog rolled out of the door. Rufus shut the door, got another glass of punch and sat back down to enjoy the music and dancing. Everyone was having the time of their life. I don't think I moved from the spot where I sat down. This nighttime stuff was for the rest of family unless it was hunting for possums or coons. Anytime there was something to hunt I went along. I remember several times the boys would bring me home sound asleep. I would doze off and that was it. I enjoyed everything we did together so I just toughed it out the best I could when we went to a party like this. I was hanging around Rufus trying to find out what made him click but that was a joke. I don't think anyone ever learned anything about Rufus.

After The Ball

Well the party was about over because it was getting late. Mama came by to see if I was all wrapped up and ready to go. The band was playing their last song and everybody was getting ready to go home. The boys were hitching up the team and the lanterns were being lit. We wouldn't burn any pine knots on the way home because it was too warm. The moon was shinning but was about to set. We all crawled into the wagon. Rufus crawled up and sat on the back of the wagon with his feet hanging off. That's all I remembered until Dad called to the mules to stop. "Whoa," he said. Rufus slid off the back of the wagon without saying a word, not even good night. Mama told Dad to wait for a minute so she could check on the children. There were five boys and three girls to check to make sure they were warm. We were a big familybut we had a good time together. There was always something to do and enjoy ourselves. Suddenly Rufus came running out of his house screaming at the top of his voice, "You all come here, something is wrong with Annie. She won't move and I can't wake her up." We all ran into the house. Annie was laying on the bed on her stomach, not moving. Dad said, "No body touch her as I believe she's dead." He ran to the wagon, took the harness of the mules and headed toward town. We waited in the wagon while Rufus sat on the steps of the house.

Soon Dad came back with the sheriff and the doctor. They went into the house. Naturally we all followed them inside. As the doctor pronounced that Annie was dead he noticed a black streak on the back of her dress. Immediately he split her dress down the back and said, "My goodness, this woman has been murdered. Everyone stand back and let the sheriff take over." Rufus grabbed his head with both hands, screamed out loud, jumped out the door and took off through the woods. The sheriff looked outside the house for any clues. Dad saw where something had dragged itself up to the door but couldn't tell anything else about it. After the sun came up we searched again and saw the marks were some-one had dug their fingers deeply into the wood. Further back from the door the tracks changed to dog claws and only the front claws. The rest of the dog had been dragged along. This told us that Annie had changed from a dog into a woman.

Rufus was never seen again and only he knew the whole story. Our family believed that Annie was a witch and Rufus did not know. But we also believed that Rufus was a warlock and did not want Annie to know. There is one thing certain, if Annie was a witch, she was a good witch. I never told anyone what I saw. But now you know.

The Return of Annie the Witch

When the doctor pronounced Annie the witch dead we all thought he knew what he was talking about. Well maybe he did, I don't know. As we waited for the sheriff, a tall young man with wide shoulders, long lanky legs, hair that was black as soot and a smile that would tempt any young girl's fantasy. A big thirty six pistol hung at his side with the holster the same color of leather as his belt. "Handsome as the devil," Mama said later as we traveled home. No one could leave until the sheriff had finished his report. As we were waiting, some one noticed one of Annie's hands moved slightly. The doctor and the sheriff spent the night sleeping on the porch at Annie's house as the coroner also had to pronounce Annie dead before either of them could leave. But that night while they were sleeping, Annie disappeared and was never found, no hide nor hair, as to say. People that knew about that night said that without a doubt her husband came back and removed her. But he never left any sign of him being there, no tracks or anything. But all of our family believe that Annie had the power to disappear or appear at anytime she chose. We believed that Annie was a witch and her husband a warlock.

The people who had seen the couple would not go anywhere near the house where they had lived nor anywhere the couple had ever been seen. People thought that something strange might happen to them. So time passed and the witch and her husband were forgotten for the most part. Not entirely though as the old house where they had lived was never touched even by the people who owned the place. They would not let anybody go near the place. Witches were the one thing that people dreaded. People everywhere believed that all witches and warlocks were bad but not Annie. No sir. My family had known Annie and her husband. We believed that they had learned to love all of us because we tried to please them and they liked it. Annie was a sweet lady with long black hair, a beautiful smile and sweet disposition. Sometimes her smiles looked different and we always looked for something to blow up like a big fire-cracker but it never did. We learned that there was no reason to take precautions, because there was no way to touch them if they refused to be touched. So we enjoyed their company when they were around. I'm sure they knew we were afraid but we never let them know for certain.

We thought about it a lot, were they really witches? They didn't look like witches but what does a witch look like? Things that happened around certainly proved to the whole family that there was something different about those two. Our dogs were very viscous but when Annie's big black dog came around our dogs nothing happened. Any other dog that came in our yard, our dogs would try to kill him or her, made no difference. People from all around have seen that big black dog many times and they wonder the same thing, why don't their dogs attack it. That big black dog seems to never changed. Just a long haired old sleepy mutt. Well if he is a mutt he's the biggest mutt I have ever seen. He always looks like he did the first time I saw him that day he came by our house a long time ago. I think of Annie and Rufus often. I like to think of them because we actually miss them being around.

My brother and I like to play in the patch of woods near the house. That was our favorite place to play and a great hideaway. We climbed trees, swung on the low limbs of the oaks trees, rode the tops of the young pines. While we were up in the tree tops we could see for miles. We were never afraid as our dogs were always with us and there was nothing to bother us anyway. There was a huge oak tree with low hanging limbs hat was fun to play on. One day it had been raining and the limbs were slick. My brother climbed up real high just to be different. His foot slipped and the other foot doubled up under him as he slid down next to the trunk of the tree. He fell over backwards as his foot caught in the new growth at one of the limbs. There was no way he could get loose. I climbed up to help. There was nothing I could do so I started home scared to death. I knew they would not let us play in the woods anymore if they saw this. I turned back and looked up at my brother to tell him that I would be back with someone to get him down. On the limb about two feet from my brother sat a beautiful lady. She had long black hair and beautiful blue eyes and a smile you would not believe. She did not speak but as I raised his head up, she helped me lift him back up on the limb. Then the growth slipped away from his foot and he started down. I looked up to thank the lady but there was no one around. The lady was gone and I did not know where. I reached the ground where my brother was and he said "where did Annie go?" I said, "who?" My brother said, "That woman was Annie the good witch. Didn't you see her? Where is she?" I replied, "I don't know but she was up there but I sure don't see her anymore. My brother said, "Look there goes that black dog. Don't tell Dad or Ma but we got someone to look after us. You ain't scared are you?" "No, I ain't scared. I'm proud of Annie even if she is a witch. I ain't scared." I answered.

From that day we watched for every day for Annie and that big black dog because we thought she always near. My brother and I never told anyone what happened. No one would have believed us anyway, so we left it alone.

The blackberries began to ripen so Mama told me and my brother to go gather some. She was planning on making blackberry jam and maybe some pies. So we got our buckets and went down to the hollow where the berries were the biggest. This was the snakiest place I have ever seen. The blackberries were as big as grapes. My brother was over to my left picking up a storm when all of a sudden he jumped and hollered out.

I couldn't see him too good but I could hear him talking to someone. I moved over and there as Annie holding a highland moccasin in her hand. She smiled as she threw the snake into the branch. My brother said, "Look at this, Annie come back here cause I want to thank you." I ran over to my brother to see what was the matter. He asked me if I had seen her. "Who?" I asked, looking from side to side. He said, "I was saw this hand go down into my berries. I thought it was you but it wasn't, it was Annie. She caught that snake that a fixing to bite me. She grabbed it by the head but she didn't hurt it. She threw it over in the creek. Boy it was close. Annie saved me again. Why didn't she speak to me or come-back so I could thank her?" I said, "I don't know. Maybe just don't want to talk to us." My brother said, "Look over there, it's that big black dog."

"Let's go home, I've been scared enough today, ain't you?" I said to my brother. "Yeah, I sure have. Reckon we ought to tell Dad about Annie and that big black dog?" he asked. "Nah, if we did Annie might stop coming to help us when we need her. We'll just let it go and we won't tell anybody."

Time passed and we always looked for Annie when we were alone. That big black dog stopped coming around like he used to. Well he might have more to do than show up for us when we are in trouble. But we know that he'll keep watch over us for Annie and we won't have to worry about that pair.

Miracle at Jasper Hollow

Annie saved our wagon, mules and maybe our lives too.

Miracle at Jasper Hollow

The rain had been pouring for three weeks now. Before that there had been a drought for over a month so we were very glad to see that rain. That morning as we awoke, the sun was shinning through the roof and the cracks in the ceiling. Everyone in the house jumped out of bed ready to do something, whatever it might be. We were not accustomed to sleeping late in the morning but there was nothing we could do in the rain, so we slept on. Today was Saturday and everyone wanted to go to town on Saturday.

Mother called us to breakfast. It was fried chicken with gravy, home-made biscuits, jelly, preserves and syrup. There was always good honey and such. Now who could sleep with that aroma floating through the house? A nice cool breeze was blowing from the north right through the house carrying the fragrance with it. Everything was just right to make a beautiful day for anyone to do anything they could wish to do.

At the breakfast table. Dad told Mama to get the kids ready and we would go into town for whatever we needed. At his remark, everyone jumped up and left the table to get ready for the trip into town. We all climbed aboard the wagon and got our seats ready for that long ride into town. Sometimes along the way, we would get off of the wagon and walk to keep the long ride from being so boring. We would sing songs together, making them up as we went along just having fun. Mama would tell us to get back into the wagon and we would sing together. Dad would always sing bass. Mama would sing the lead and we would join in and sing whatever part that we could do.

Everyone quieted down as we looked ahead at the low land just before we were to cross the bridge at muddy creek. The bottom land and the road was covered with water. We could seethe top rails on the bridge so we knew that the bridge was still there. The mules did not slow down as if they knew that everything was all right. So we kept on going. The water was awful swift. My brother and I were holding on to our big brothers overall legs just in case. The girls all curled up in a little circle in the middle of the wagon. Dad and Mama wasn't saying anything until Mama said, "Hadn't we better turn back?" Dad told Mama that we could not turn back as the road was too narrow and the wagon might turn over and we would all drown. "Oh Lord," Mama said as she gnawed on her fist. Dad just held on to the reins as the mules continued on.

As the bridge got closer. Dad told all of us to lay down in the middle of the wagon so that the wagon would not be top heavy and hold on. As we started across the bridge the wagon was on the planks of the bridge then all of a sudden one wheel of the wagon went down about a foot with a bang. The whole family screamed as the mules stopped dead still. Dad didn't know what to do. He was afraid for one of the grown boys to get off because the current was so strong that they might drown. Dad called to the mules but they never moved. The water seemed to be rising by the minute. The team would not move. Dad was afraid to strike the mules for they might panic and hurt themselves or turn the wagon over. Then we all might drown or at least be in a bad shape.

My brother raised his head and looked at the team, then he nudged me and said, "Look, there's that big black dog standing in front of the mules, just off the bridge where there was no water. It's just looking at Pa. I'm scared." "Me too." I answered. "What's that big black dog up to?" my brother asked. "I don't know. Maybe we'll see soon enough," I told him.

That big black dog waded out in the water, looked the mules straight in the eyes just as if he was saying something to them. He then turned around and started slowly back out of the water but the mules did nothing. The dog looked back, turned around and gave the saddest howl I have ever heard till this very day. As the dog turned. Dad tapped the mules with the reins and the mules started slowly off. The wagon seemed like it was lifted up by some unknown power. My brother and I still say that was Annie that raised up that wheel and helped us get that wagon off that bridge. The big black dog led them mules to the end of that bridge cause that bridge was crooked where the water went down.

We went home another way late that evening. Dad and Mama never mentioned that big black dog but my brother and I know, we just know Annie and her dog helped us get out of there cause there was nobody else around for miles. We don't know what happened with the big black dog but I'm sure he is still around waiting and watching for us to need him to help us.

Annie Goes Hiking

Annie is still helping the lost and helpless.

Annie Goes Hiking

Many years have now passed since Annie the good witch played a part in my life. I thought she was forgotten many years ago. Seems like they never forget the ones they love. Believe me they can love like anybody else. Annie the good witch has proved that time after time and I always recognize her no matter what.

The Boy Scout troop which I was leading was getting ready to go hiking. The troop wanted to go on a hike in a large area at the foot of a mountain. The mountain was a long way off but they wanted to go across the wooded area to get to the foot of the mountain. I told the boys that it would take some time to cross the area between the two points which they had suggested. Oh that was all right with all of them. I told them if that is what you want then start getting ready. Pack enough foot and drink to last for several days. I was trying to discourage them but I was wasting my time. The territory was very rough and swampy but that was all right, let's go. Well there was nothing to do but take them.

Everyone packed his bag with his own water supply and food and was ready for the trip early in the morning. The weather was hot and humid with flies of all kinds, mosquitoes, ticks and ant that we knew would be bad so we came prepared.

Off we started, everyone having a good time. The sun went down awful quick behind that mountain. It got dark real early so we stopped for supper. We sat down for a while and got acquainted with the area before we got ready to eat. We cleared a large place and built several fires. We heated up our supperof soup or whatever had been brought. After we ate we sat around telling tales and singing songs. Some of the stories would have scared the devil if he had been there but no he wasn't there just us scouts.

We turned in early so we would rise early the following morning. We arose about the same time the sun did the next morning, had breakfast and headed out. We looked at the mountain and it seemed to be backwards to where it was supposed to be but we traveled on toward the mountain.

We did not mark the trail. Why anybody would have know the mountain was in front of us. Or was it? I know how to maneuver in any type of land, forest or wilderness. Well I thought I could. Maybe that's why it is named Lost Mountain. It may not be lost but it sure lost us. Of course we just got turned around, that's what happened. (I think) Another day passed, we had supper and went to bed.

We awoke with the sunrise. It had begun to rain, a slow drizzle which made it hard on us but we carried on. About the middle of the day, we stopped to eat a bite. Everybody was tired of walking and realizing it was a long way back, suggested that we turn back. So we turned back or some other way, we never quite figured it out, but we turned back.

Our food and water was almost gone. Some of the boys had no water or food left. But no one complained. We thought we were headed back to where we had left our bus but after three and a half days, no one was sure. We weren't worried because we knew somebody would find us but no one knew which way we went so how could we be found? We came to a large creek which looked like a good place to fish. We needed food of some kind to eat. The first time the hook hit the water baited with a piece of a hot dot that one of the boys still had, someone caught a huge brown trout. We caught enough fish that we ad a big fish fry.

I have never been so full of fish and felt so good about it in my life. The next morning we fished some more and had trout for breakfast. We started on our way again following that stream. Mile after mile we walked. When we got hungry we caught more fish. Now after a while those fish got hard to swallow. I am glad we had plenty of salt to go on our fish. With it we could have not eaten many more. I guess we should be thankful that we found that stream as it probably saved our lives. I still can not eat fish this day, oh well, maybe some day. We spent night after night by that stream because we knew where our meals were coming from. We were lost all right but we thought that stream would cross a road or path of some kind somewhere but it never happened.

We were seriously exhausted, several of the boys just wanted to sit down and die. They were tired of walking, in fact they were tired of living. As long as we had food to eat and water to drink, I did not worry about stopping to rest when we got tired. There was a lot to worry about besides food and water. There was always the possibility of snake bites, sickness or even coming upon some animal that might attack one of us.

One morning we came to an opening in the forest, it was just a small clearing. Out about ten yards stood the biggest bear I have ever seen. Of course that bear was the biggest bear in the world from our point of view a wild squirrel would have been a large as a wolf if we thought he was going to attack us. I knew this was the end for me and if I went the others would surely starve or panic or shucks I could think of a thousand things that might happen with or without me. The bear even looked like meat for us to eat but how could we shoot him? We did not have a gun. Even if we had a gun we wouldn't have shot him anyway. The bear just strolled off like we weren't even there. We just walked on. I guess no one was frightened but me but no one mentioned it.

I'll tell anybody that I did not know what to do. That mountain was still in the same place as it was to start with. The boys were getting weary and tired. Some seemed to be a little sick. Everything was going wrong. Something had to happened pretty soon.

I awoke early one morning. The sun was shining, the sky was clear, it was a beautiful day. I looked on the other side of the stream and there was a girl that seemed to be fishing. She seemed to be twenty-three or twenty-four years old. I walked over to where I could see her and talk to her. Maybe she could tell us the way out of here. I hollered out to her if she could tell is which way to go. She said, "See those rocks in the stream?" I answered, "Yes, I do." She said, "Then cross the stream and go straight ahead. You don't want to go any further the way you are going." So I got the boys up and urged them to get ready quick. As I packed my things together I realized that was Annie the good witch.

I threw down my things and ran back to the place where the woman was fishing. She never looked up this time. I said, with a smile in my heart, "We thank you, Annie." Annie looked up and smiled. Someone called me from behind and asked, "What did you say? And who are you talking to? I don't see anyone." I said that I was just singing a little song. Thank you Lord for saving my soul. They all joined in and we sang along as we crossed the stream. About four hours we walked. I knew not to go back to that stream because Annie had told me not to go any further in that direction.

One of the boys screamed out with joy when he saw the roof of a house a long way off. When we reached the house, a man came out and told us that someone was looking for a troop of scouts who had gotten lost. He said that he lived up the road about a mile. He didn't know the man as he had only lived here a short time. Well right up the road is where we left out bus to get out. Boys, looks like we are back home again. Did everyone have fun? They all said, "Yeah, yeah."   But I knew they were lying.

Strange Encounter

A young man meets the girl of his dreams. She is willing but circum-
stances control her life The young mans love lives forever in his heart.

STRANGE ENCOUNTER

The band was playing a beautiful love song as I danced across the floor. The most beautiful girl I had ever seen was in my arms. This night was made especially for me. I had just been elected sheriff of the county and I was celebrating my twenty-eighth birthday. All of this was almost too much for me at the same time.

As the band played "After the Ball" the lady asked me to sit this one out, so we did. As we sat there I introduced myself and so did she. "My name is Paul, Paul Winslow" as I looked straight into the most loving, bluest eyes I had ever seen. Her lips were so soft looking, my heart pounded like a jack hammer and I was afraid to even look too hard at her much less touch her. She said with a gleam in those beautiful eyes, "My name is Katie". She smiled and looked down at the floor. "That's a lovely name", I said but she interrupted. "It is not." She continued to smile. I asked if I could take her home as I had a buggy. "Oh yes", she said, "I saw you pass my house on your way here, I'm sure father won't mind, he is such a politician." "Well, maybe he will learn to like me, I truly hope so," I replied. Everyone came by to shake my hand and offer congratulations on my new job. I was very happy. After everyone had left the band played "After the Ball" once more and we danced together. It was awesome.

We reached her house about midnight. Her father and mother were on the porch waiting. I thought they were going to chew me out but no they were proud that I had driven her home. They said good night and I drove away in my pretty buggy with my high stepping horse. Paint holding her head high in the cool night breeze. Suddenly I stopped the horse and just sat there like a nut. I said to myself, "Paul, you are so crazy, you didn't even touch that girl much less kiss those pretty lips. No I didn't, "I replied back to myself. But I was happy. I continued on down the road whistling and humming "After the Ball".

My duties were hard and being sheriff was wan all day job. Usually I did not get home until well after dark since I had to go about nine miles to get home. Katie would also be waiting to wave at me as I passed by her house.

I was really interested in this beautiful girl so I made every effort to see her that I could. Late one afternoon I had papers to deliver to gentleman to appear in court. I had to pass by Katie's house as I traveled to the man's house. Katie and her parents were working in the yard so I stopped to say hello. We all talked for a while then I asked her parents if I could come courting Katie. Strangely enough, they all agreed almost in unison that I should come courting on Saturday evening.

hat Saturday night I got there early. I rode old Paint who wasn't really old, I just called her that. We had a wonderful time just having fun, talking, eating and just plain courting. As I was leaving, she walked me to the edge of the porch. I stopped and looked at her in the light of the lamp shinning through the door of the hall. I felt the strings of my heart playing music. "Katie," I said in a trembling voice, "could I kiss you, good night?" She put her arms behind her back and leaned forward. I kissed her on her soft lips. This was the greatest kiss of my life. Right then I knew I had to have her. I asked her to marry me and she accepted.

We began planning the wedding for next June. It seemed along way off but her parents insisted. This would allow us enough time to take care of the plans and setting up housekeeping. All I wanted was for Katie to be my wife.

One Saturday night I want to Katie's house as usual. The previous Saturday night I had to break our date as I had to go pick up a prisoner in the next county. As I walked up the porch Katie's mother met me with a gloomy look on her face. At the time I couldn't understand. Katie's mother had told me about her sister in South Carolina and that Katie had gone to visit her. Katie had taken the train yesterday. I could not understand why Katie did not stop by the office and tell me that she was going. As I usually met the train to ensure the safety of the people traveling to and from our town, I had not seen Katie. I know I would have seen her. I did not ask her mother any more questions but walked away. I thought that maybe Katie had gotten mad at me as I had broken a date with her but I thought she understood that my job would have to come first. That was simply part of being the sheriff. Oh well, what the heck, she should be back in no time at all. I knew Katie love me as much as I loved her. She could hardly wait from one Saturday to the next. This had never happened. Her parents did not ask me to visit them during her absence. So I tried not to think of her but she was on my mind every minute of every day, now and then. All I have of Katie are fond memories.

Time passed but I never heard again from Katie. My world seemed to crumble around me as I thought only of Katie. I had to put her from my mind and concentrate on my job. There was always somebody watching for the sheriff to blunder even slightly. So I want on the best that I could. When a man fell in love in those days it was forever. I thought I could get her out of my mind but I had too many questions. Each night as I passed her house my heart broke a little further. I had given Katie a beautiful engagement ring with the biggest diamond I had ever seen but she only wore it on our Saturday evenings. She loved that diamond almost as much as she love me. I never heard anything more from her parents.

Several years passed by, but still no word or sign of Katie. What had happened to my love? I couldn't understand it. I knew it was all over for me as far as love went. I could never love another woman like I did Katie. I heard word that Katie had married someone in South Carolina. I could not believe that no matter who told me.

Late one evening storm clouds started moving into the area. I could tell that a big storm was brewing. I tried to get home before the storm struck but I was not that lucky. Lightening flashed, thunder roared and the wind blew very hard. One bolt of lightening struck after another. This was the worst storm I had ever seen. I stopped Paint up close to the front of a small church. The House of Jeremiah had a small porch across the front. I dismounted and tied Paint to the rail. I opened the door and stepped inside the building. As I wiped the rain from my face I glanced toward the front of the church. As the lightening flashed I could see a figure climbing over the wooden pews toward the rear of the church. Whoever or whatever steadily climbed over one pew at time toward me. I wondered who would be climbing over the pews in a church during a terrible storm. It was too dark to see who or what it was. I decided that when whatever reached the last pew I was going outside. I went outside and untied Paint. As I was swinging up into the saddle I felt someone or something mount behind me. Paint, sensing my fear and feeling the extra weight, took off like a ball shot out of a cannon. I couldn't hold her back as the rain and hail hit us. I couldn't see because long black hair was blowing over my face. I did not know who was behind me, it would have been the devil for all I knew. But a devil would not come out a church, would it? I looked down to see what was nearly squeezing the breath out of my body. I saw the pretty smooth white hand of a woman. On the left hand there was a large diamond that I had placed on Katie's finger a longtime ago. I knew then that this creature that held me so closely as we rode through the storm was the only girl I had ever loved. I did not say a word, just smiled as the storm was nearly over. I slowed Paint down to a slow trot. When we reached Katie's home, she still had never spoken a word. I pulled up to the porch. Katie's mother and father came to door and helped Katie down. They led her into the house. As I rode away with tears streaming down my face, my heart broke again. All my hope was gone but now at least I knew what had happened to Katie. She had not married another man but had been taken to an asylum. Katie had lost her mind. Her family had not wanted to tell me as they knew how much it would hurt.

Katie's father told me later, "Son, we did not know how to tell you this had happened. We knew you would be deeply hurt. We thought maybe she would get better with treatment and you could have become our son in law."

Dog Named Mame

A strange sick dog, comes into a young boys life. The boy has doubts
and and fear for the dog. As days go by, they become best of friends. The
dog proved, to be a best friend.

Dog Named Mame

School was out and there was no one around to play with. I was getting bored having nothing to do. I had no pets as I didn't like animals at
al. This was the beginning of my second week of loneliness. I was only
eight years old. I had been going to school every day and I loved it. The
school was very nice and all the kids were nice to me. So when school was
out I was lonesome. I was always hunting something to do but finding
nothing.

My father and I were sitting on the porch of the house where I lived
with my father and mother. A swing which Dad had made and hung on
the porch was very comfortable. It was plenty big enough for the two of
us and we loved to spend time just swinging. Mother was doing the
dinner dishes. The day was lazy and somewhat hot, in fact I was about to
take a good old summer nap when this ugly, sick looking, mange eaten
old dog came up to the porch and just looked at Dad and me. The dog
looked as if he was about to starve to death. I don't think he had eaten in
several days. His sores were running all over his body. I felt sick to my
stomach. I couldn't hardly stand to look at him.

"Dad," I said and he answered "Yes, son?" I said, "Dad, goin the house
and get your gun and shoot that mangy old dog." Dad stopped swinging and looked at me. "Well son," he said, "you know how to shoot the
gun, you go get the gun and shoot that dog yourself. He's just an old sick
dog. Go right ahead and kill that poor dog."

Dad knew all the time that I couldn't kill that dog or any other animal.
But that dog made me feel sick. I asked Dad to shoo the dog away and he
told me to do it myself. "No Dad", I said, "I don't want to go near that
dog." Dad loved animals of any kind and he didn't want to get attached

to the dog.

Just then Mother came out and saw the dog. She said "Oh, what a poor sick old dog. Leave here quick!", clapping her hands together. The dog ran under the house. Suddenly the dog began to holler and howl. I jumped off the porch and got down on my knees to look under the house. "Oh Dad, the dog is stuck under the porch, help me get it out."

"Well Son," Dad said, "I thought you wanted me to kill that dog." "Dad, please help me get him loose, he's stuck." Dad said to stop hollering and crawl under the house. I looked at Dad then at the crying dog. I crawled under the porch and got the dog out. That mangy dog then licked me. I didn't know what I felt now. Mother went into the house and brought out the scraps from the meal. That dog was certainly glad to gulp down some food.

We talked about what might be wrong with the dog and Dad fixed some sulfur and water to bath him in to treat the sores. After I had washed him good we rubbed him all over with burnt motor oil to help the sores and the dog looked a lot better.

The day was coming to an end as we finished with the dog. Even Dad and Mother helped. I went to the barn and got an old quilt to fix the dog a pallet to lay on to sleep. I never did find out where the dog had come from. At that time there were a lot of stray dogs running wild, he might have been one of them.

During the night I went out to check on the dog. I guess I checked on him because I didn't want to lose him. I sneaked out some more food scraps from the kitchen. I knew right then that I had me a brand new friend. He was so proud that some one loved him. I was worried about him leaving at first but I soon realized that he was not going anywhere.

While watching a show on TV I heard the name of one of the characters was Mame. I didn't worry about whether he was a boy or girl, I just liked the name, so I named the dog Mame. Everyone called him Mame until the day he left us.

One day when I was about fourteen years old, I went on a trip with some friends. We brought Mame along. We went to a huge lake. Next door to the people we were visiting was a young girl. She was sitting on the dock where the boats were tied. Mame I strolled down there to see what she was doing. She was just sitting there so we began talking. While we were sitting there the girl's cat came down to join us. Strangely enough the cat was not afraid of Mame. Mame looked the cat over. Oh boy, I thought, I'm in trouble now. Mame's hair stood straight up on his back, his lips tightened over his gums and his mouth was open as if he was going to eat that cat. Neither the girl, Katie, or I spoke. We just sat there waiting to see what was going to happen. Mame's hair finally laid down and he realized everything was all right. That cat walked over the Katie, rubbed her head on her leg and walked right over the Mame and rubbed her head on Mame's head. Mame opened his mouth and licked the cat. For once, I didn't know what to do. All of a sudden a huge bat came speeding by the dock. The wake of the boat cause the dock to raise high and fall which caused the cat to fall into the water. Katie screamed "Please help me get my cat. I can't swim." "Oh," I said, "I can't either." What would we do? We were both screaming for help. Well of course the cat could swim. I guess he could because he was going round and round. We just kept on screaming but no one came to help. Mame stood up, went to the edge of the dock whining and shaking head, then jumped off the dock, swam over to the cat and caught him by the back of his head. He then swam to the shore and climbed out. He then proudly brought the cat to Katie and gently laid it down. Katie was so happy she petted Mame a long time. After she dried off the cat, we became great friends. For years we visited each other. Katie and I, with our animals, had lots of fun.

Time passed so fast, Mame grew old and began to lose weight. We couldn't get him to eat at all. Mame was just getting old; we knew that. The veterinarian said there was nothing he could do for him. One morning I woke to hear Mame whining and grunting but when I reached him, he had passed away. My heart almost stopped but there was nothing no one could do. It was just time for him to go. Dad helped me put him away in a place where his grave would not be disturbed. We dug his grave with a flat shovel which we decided to make a grave marker out of. We took it to the blacksmith shop where I held it on the anvil and Dad took a round end punch and dented placed in it. These indents would be plain to see. We put a heavy iron handle into the shovel so it would last forever. At the head of Mame's grave we dug adeep hole, placed the shovel in it and firmly packed the dirt around it. The words were plain to see on the marker, HERE LIES MAME. Mame was never forgotten by any of the family. I have never had a more friendly animal and to this day I still think of my dog, Mame.

About the Author

Adell Digby is one of nine children. He has been married to Sarah McGiboney since 1929. He and Sarah have four children and several grandchildren and great-grandchildren.

Printed in the United States
1494500001B/394-435